THE SHIPWRIGHT
& OTHER STORIES

THE SHIPWRIGHT
& OTHER STORIES

Matthew Buscemi

Published by Matthew Buscemi, 2020
Seattle, Washington USA

ISBN 978-1-62802-022-9

Typeset by Matthew Buscemi in Apollo with Optimus Princeps display

TABLE OF CONTENTS

THE SHIPWRIGHT

A bireme drifted lazily across the sea beyond Arkh's window. He tapped his pencil rhythmically and absently against the tabletop, and jolted when the the tip of the lead cracked and splintered, leaving a blotch of grey and a spray of fallout shards atop his design documents. He turned his attention, grumbling, away from the sea and toward the mess upon his desk.

A slap on his shoulder jerked at his attention yet again. Fíl stood over his shoulder, smirking. "Didn't take you for a Kholumvite grunt."

Arkh silently chastised himself for being so lost in thought he hadn't even heard his friend enter the guild.

He chortled as he picked up his waste bin and began brushing the splinters away. "You ever seen a regiment of the aquatic legion?"

Fíl crossed his arms. "No, but I know you have. Remind me again how awesome the big city is."

"Kholumvite swimmers are agile and graceful. Swimming is not a brute force kind of sport."

"Speaking of sports..." Fíl motioned to the window, indicating the sun, which had passed below the mountains, dimming their view of the sea. The mountaintop glowed bright yellow, soon to morph through the rest of the spectrum. "How about a run?"

Fond memories of their lessons with Master Anatix, especially the races, flitted back to Arkh, and he grinned. Then he looked at the mess on his desk and sighed. "Let me just finish this up real quick."

"Can I help?"

"Sure."

Fíl pulled a stool up to Arkh's workbench while Arkh scratched away the lead blot as best he could. Then, together, the two of them went over Arkh's design documents. One paper held the measurements of each plank, while another contained sketches of planks and their fittings, all drawn as precisely as possible. A steady hand was of utmost importance. He'd been stupid to break the lead.

Arkh retrieved his ruler from the drawer beside his bench and began measuring lines while Fíl called out the numbers from the other paper.

"This is supposed to be a bireme, right?" Fíl interjected halfway through the list.

"Yeah," Ark said.

"Isn't it a bit long for that?"

"We're trying out a new design."

Fíl shrugged. "Sure."

Arkh sensed his friend was leaving something unsaid. "What is it?"

"Well…" Fíl made the uncomfortable fidgeting motions typical of him when he was trying not to fidget. "I think you're going to have all the usual trouble I hear they're having with those prototype triremes. You know, too slow to turn, too vulnerable in the middle, etcetera, etcetera."

Arkh blinked at him a few times. "This is shorter than those. It's a bireme."

Fíl held up his hands. "I'm just sayin'."

Arkh sighed. "Let's go for that run."

The outline of the mountain had turned bright red.

Fíl stood and kicked his stool under Arkh's workbench with a swift swipe of his foot. Arkh returned his supplies to their appropriate shelves and drawers, and placed his stool underneath his bench as well. He then joined Fíl by the door, where he grabbed up the long strips of clothes hanging from the peg with his name etched into the wood above it. He lifted his right foot first, like always, and began wrapping the cloth around it.

Fíl had already finished wrapping both his feet, and was now removing his yellow-dyed merchant's robes. He hung them on the visitor's peg where his foot wrappings had been. Arkh hurried to finish his other other foot and removed his navy-blue robes, the robes of a shipwright.

Arkh closed the door to the guild behind them and latched it shut. Out of habit, he visually scanned the windows, too.

The two of them, now wearing only loincloths, jogged down the deserted country road to the lone tree at the intersection of the guild road and the road into the city. A light breeze passed over the island, and the clouds were light and wispy in the sky. Very few of them, too. They'd get a good view of Khatap tonight.

They reached the intersection, also deserted. The last of Arkh's colleagues had retired for home over an hour ago.

Arkh stretched his arms above his head while Fíl stretched his legs.

"You go running at all while you were in Épanngel?" Fíl asked.

"Nah," Arkh said. "Didn't have time."

Fíl smirked. "Should be an easy win for me then."

"You wish," Arkh shot back.

"Ready?" Fíl took up his starting pose.

Arkh nodded and knelt as well.

"Set," Arkh said.

"Go!" Fíl shouted.

Arkh took off, his feet pounding across the dirt road. They ran away from the city, eastward toward Khatap's meager mountains, more like large hills. Funny how he understood that now. Khatap's mountains had always seemed mountainous before, but then he'd visited Épanngel and seen those towering behemoths in the distance, jagged peaks that spanned the entire western horizon beyond the city. Khatap's rounded stumps upon which races could be run had not seemed so mountainous after that.

At first, Arkh kept pace with Fíl easily, but as they began their ascent, Arkh indeed wondered if he should have kept up with his exercise during his recent trip.

There hadn't been much helping it. The trip by boat from Khatap to Épanngel took eight days each way, and even on large passenger boats, the opportunities for exercise had been limited. He'd sufficed with push ups and crunches. Only slaves rowed.

Lost in his memories of the big city, Arkh didn't notice the large ash tree near the peak until Fíl began surging past him. Arkh pushed as hard he could, but he was too late. Fíl crossed the finish line with just a couple of mettrs on him.

They both slowed and panted. Fíl took to stretching, while Arkh meandered over to the precipice. He sat, his legs hanging and swinging over the edge. It was indeed a beautiful evening. Stathro sat just above the city, its dull blue reflecting against the darkening water, while Atax hovered above and slightly behind them, granting the scene a maroon backlight. It would be a bright evening, and Khatap proper glowed like a tiny red-blue gem on the great ocean when these two moons were out and Isórrop hid. The white glow of the third and largest moon would drown out the red and blue of its smaller siblings when present. But Isórrop was illuminating other lands tonight.

Arkh's mind drifted back to his work. The Guild Master would complain that Arkh hadn't finished the preliminaries of the new bireme, but the run had been worth it. He didn't know how many more of these sprints he was going to get.

"What do your parents think?" Fíl stood at his side.

Arkh shrugged. "Dad changed the subject when I told him about it. Mom's already bragging to all her friends about how her son's going to get a job in Épann-gel."

"How did you come from them?" Fíl sat down at the precipice beside Arkh. He'd long ago learned that criticizing Arkh's parents was fair game.

"No clue." Arkh picked up a stone and chucked it off the precipice. It took a long dive, hundreds of mettrs down. The sound of its landing was inaudible, eaten by the conifers below, perhaps.

"You really want this, don't you?"

Arkh nodded. "Yeah, I do." He let out a long sigh.

"This guild is so… Methís is a drunk. Ilik is too old to read fine writing anymore, and the Guild Master is—"

Arkh stopped himself.

Fíl looked out across Khatap, silently.

Arkh began again. "They're good people. They've been especially good to me. Sure better than most other adults in my life."

"Hey, don't forget about Anatix," Fíl reminded him.

Arkh smiled. "I'll miss you and him the most."

Fíl punched him in the shoulder. He opened his mouth, then closed it. The light faded from his eyes, and he looked back at their tiny, blue-red city.

"What?" Arkh asked.

Fíl waited a long time, then took a deep breath and said. "You're gonna get it, Arkh."

"What do you mean?"

"C'mon, really? Who helped who with all of Anatix's insane math problems? Who helped who measure the time from our shadows? And who read half of that book of Sófan geometry the first night after Anatix assigned it? I couldn't have figured out half this stuff without you. I don't think I'd have learned it. You'll get that position for sure."

"You don't give yourself enough credit."

Fíl chortled. "Whatever, man."

"It's not decided yet."

"There's probably already a courier ship on its way here right now. Think of it. Sailing across the Messig right now is your acceptance letter."

Arkh wasn't sure how to reply to that. He really wanted the position in Épanngel, but he also hadn't let himself think about how he and Fíl would be parting ways. Mostly he dreamed of shedding his family. A word of encouragement that Fíl too could achieve a job in Épanngel flitted through his mind, but the words were quickly quashed by the harsh reality that Fíl had lost his father eight years ago, and Fíl's mother was now entirely dependent upon his income. Moving to the mainland was simply not an option for him.

"Tell me about the aquatic legion," Fíl suggested.

Arkh laughed. "I thought you were sick of hearing about them."

Fíl smiled. "Tell me again."

Arkh and Fíl sat atop the mountain, Arkh first telling stories of the big city, and then later they reminisced about their years of tutelage under Anatix, who'd been a father to both of them at various times and in various ways—Arkh because his father was too busy to be bothered with any matter concerning his son, and Fíl after his father had been lost to him.

They shared stories for many hours, until the red and blue glows were the sole illumination in the sky. The old stories called such nights 'Métav, the time of upheaval.' Métav had, at one time, held strong religious significance, but those beliefs were ancient. Modern religions put more faith in specific gods than the moons' light.

Arkh found his mind drifting back to the ancient stories. The bard had told them many times on festival nights. Arkh ran them through his mind as he and Fíl hurtled back down the mountain path. Could the force of Métav be pushing an acceptance letter across the Messig right now? It would upheave his life, certainly. He smiled at the thought.

'Never presume that you will find favor with the gods,' Anatix had told him once.

'Why?' a twelve-year-old Arkh had asked.

'The gods have a way of thwarting your intentions when you ask their help in seeking what you covet.'

'How?'

'By giving it to you.'

Arkh had not known what Anatix had meant at the time. But now he had seen Épanngel. For three days, he'd walked those busy streets, seen those towering stone structures, some of them dozens of mettrs tall. He'd witnessed artwork in galleries and eaten at dining halls more elaborately decorated than the city council chambers of Khatap.

When he really asked himself, deep down, how he felt about Épanngel, there was something else, besides excitement, besides yearning. But he couldn't tell Fíl. It would hurt him, and Arkh couldn't do that to such a good friend.

As nice as it would be to get away from his family

and to have a real career, Arkh knew he was a country boy at heart. He knew nothing of the politics and the culture of Épanngel, or any of Palípoli's other major cities. Until a month ago, Khatap had circumscribed and his entire life.

As they hurtled through the dark shadows of trees and the intermittent red-blue glow of the moons, Arkh realized their would be no after-dark marathons with friends, should he find any, in Épanngel.

One did not risk a foray out into the nighttime streets of such a large city.

Arkh rolled out of bed the next morning feeling groggy and disoriented. He stumbled across the floorboards, the pre-dawn glow just barely reaching into his room. Frigid wind screamed through the slits in his windows. It was still summer, and so there was no frost, but even during the summer, the nights and mornings on Khatap could get quite cold.

A sailor had once told him that the coastal cities of Palípoli had less moderate climates than the islands, with colder winters and warmer summers. The worst, he'd said, was Apmonómen, a city far to the northwest build inland from the coast. They protected themselves by using their river as a natural fortification on three sides. A small port town on the coast facilitated naval trade, and all disembarking visitors had to travel three days by foot from the port town to the city proper. Their landlocked winters, he'd said, were the harshest in the region, with snow that actually clung to the ground for days, and would melt and refreeze multiple times before the spring months arrived.

For all Arkh's fascination with designing and building ships, he found the act of traveling by boat unsettling, mostly because he knew how prone to defects their designs were. He considered it a miracle of the gods that ships functioned at all. He'd shared this observation only with Fíl.

Arkh threw on his robes, pulled open the hatch in the floor, and dropped a rope ladder down into the hall. The house was still quiet, but his parents would wake soon. He hurried down the hall and toward the staircase that led to the first floor, then out into the cold morning and toward the bathhouse.

He filled the basin and lit the logs, which had been set out for him the previous night by his home's servants. He could see them, already moving about the fields and within the barn. His father, thanks to lucrative investments in his youth, owned two fields in addition to that barn. They could feed themselves and all the service in a good year, and stock enough to suffice in poorer years. Khatap had always been a good island for farming, from what he'd heard.

As Arkh knelt over the warmth of the growing fire underneath the basin, he wondered if he would want to stay if his parents genuinely cared about him more. He decided eventually that the opportunity offered by Épanngel would have enticed him away regardless. He simply loved math and geometry and drawing out ship designs too much.

He stripped off his robes and loincloth, and, shivering, slipped into the bathtub, where he washed away all the worries of the previous night.

By the time he was dressed, the sun had peaked up over the sea, or perhaps the ocean. It was hard to say what it was that Khatap port sat against. No one had ever discovered any land to the east of Khatap. All that was known were the great lands to the west and the other islands of Palípoli to the north. The ship that had gone out the farthest east from Khatap had been a huge, gilded Meigánite bireme, which had returned after two weeks away from port. The ship's navigator had calculated their voyage at six hundred and thirty thousand mettrs, almost the distance between Khatap and Épanngel. They had seen nothing but water the entire way.

Perhaps Khatap lay in a huge sea, or perhaps the water went on forever to the end of the world. Many captains believed their ships might fall off the world's edge if they sailed too far out. Not the Meigánites, it seemed.

Arkh remained convinced that either more land or more water lay beyond his home. He doubted the gods would be so capricious as to allow the world to simply end. Besides, how would the sea level rise and fall like it did if its volume were constantly spilling off some precipice into void? That didn't make sense either.

He grabbed an apple and a loaf of bread from the larder adjacent to the kitchen, threw on his dark blue shipwright robes, and hurried out the door. He was glad to have missed his parents this morning.

He strode down the path from his home to the fence that demarcated his family's property and let himself out the gate, re-latching it as he left. He broke into a jog down the main road.

Traffic was sparse. He passed a few farmers and shepherds, but that was all. His house lay at the very edge of the city boundaries, a very good chunk of land. The guild where Arkh worked lay outside the city limits, like most guilds he knew of. Except Fíl's merchant's guild. They wanted to be at the center of commerce, of course.

Arkh recalled the first time he'd visited the Shipwright's Guild. Anatix had learned of Arkh's interest in ship designs and had introduced him personally to the Guild Master, who turned out to be one of Anatix's old friends. One of Arkh's first questions had been, 'Why isn't the guild closer to the shipyard?'

To which the Guild Master had responded, 'Builders need tools and a place to build. For the builder following the design, the tools are wood, wax, and hammers, and the place is a dock. For the builder *of* the design, the tools are pencils and paper, and the place is somewhere quiet, where he can concentrate.'

Anatix had then encouraged Arkh to listen more before asking questions, and Arkh had since thought more carefully about his questions before voicing them.

He approached the guild, which looked much as he had left it, the front door closed and latched shut. That surprised him. Even when Arkh came directly to work, he wasn't usually the first one in. The Guild Master arrived very early.

Arkh pulled open the door, took off his foot wrappings, and hung them up.

"Hello?" he called into the vacant building.

No response.

He meandered through the stuffy room, weaving around workbenches, until he came to his desk. He pulled open the window beside it, allowing the warming breeze of morning to flood the space, evacuating staleness.

He pulled out his stool, sat, and frowned.

Where was everyone?

A thought struck him.

He pulled open his drawer and pulled out his calendar.

Of course. He'd forgotten that it was Chryday. Everyone was in town picking up their guild salary from the council hall.

Arkh decided to take the opportunity to finish up the bireme design before his coworkers arrived. Perhaps he could eke out the final calculations and not be late with them after all. He pulled out his pencils, his ruler, and his compass and got to work.

The sounds of birds singing and waves crashing against the shore from beyond his window faded away. His mind honed in on the equations and measurements before him, and his pen transcribed the mathematical drama that played out within his mind.

The sound of the door and Ilik's voice broke his trance. He could hear the Guild Master, too.

He was nearly done with his initial design, but not quite. Arkh refocused on his task, and scrawled lines, diagrams and measurements even faster than before.

The muffled clink of metal sounded at his side, and Arkh jumped.

"Still at it?" The guild master stood over his workbench, his hand retracting from the small purse of coins he left atop the desk's surface.

Arkh gulped. "It's nearly complete, Master."

"Let me see." The Guild Master moved around to Arkh's side of the workbench, and Arkh arranged all his papers so that everything would be visible.

"This will be weak in the middle and difficult to maneuver, like the trireme designs we got from Sóf last year."

"I thought so, too, Master. But the specification from the council says it must be thirty-five mettrs long."

The Guild Master nodded morosely. "Yes. I find it sad that we still receive specifications for specific lengths, specific heights, specific oars, specific sails. Khatap pays us because we are the experts. They should tell us which problems they wish us to solve. If we lived in that Sófan teacher's ideal world, that is how it would be. But the workings of men are far removed from the workings of the gods. Speaking of which..." The Guild Master stabbed at one of Arkh's measurements. "This length here does not match the length of its corresponding plank here."

Indeed. Arkh had incorrectly copied the decimal place. He hurriedly began scratching out the mistake and recalculating all the other equations that utilized its result. The Guild Master loomed over him still.

Arkh did his best to remain as calm as could, but could not help but wonder why the Guild Master remained at his side. Was the Guild Master judging him? Perhaps Arkh's mistake had meant that the Guild Master would write a letter to Épanngel telling them he was unfit to take a job in the big city. He'd been eerily silent and calm when Arkh had told the Guild Master his intentions. Perhaps he didn't approve...?

Arkh hurried through the calculations.

"Careful..." The Guild Master said.

Arkh looked over his most recent calculation.

Idiot. He'd made a simple multiplication mistake, the mistake of a child.

Why did the Guild Master have to be hovering over him?

On and on Arkh went, growing ever more nervous and having to force himself to take the math slowly.

Finally, after what seemed like an eternity, he reached the end of his recalculations. He took a deep breath, and turned to look at the Guild Master. The Guild Master's face was stony, and Arkh's heart fell.

"A question," the Guild Master said.

Arkh nodded. 'Here it comes,' he thought. 'He's going to tell me I shouldn't go to Épanngel.'

"How many repercussions did your early error have?"

Arkh blinked. "I'm sorry, Master. I don't quite understand your question."

The Guild Master nodded gently and grinned. "How many equations did you have to recalculate due to the one mistake?"

Arkh turned back to his papers. They all seemed a grey-white blur, even though he had drawn and composed them himself. Slowly, he fixed his eyes on the original scratched out blot and drew his gaze across all the others, counting them as he went.

"Sixteen," Arkh said.

"And, if you had found the error this morning when you arrived, how many do you think you would have had to correct?"

Arkh looked at his papers again. "Perhaps... four or five."

"And if you had recognized the error as soon as it

occurred, how many equations would have required re-calculation?"

Arkh worried he was being trapped in a trick question. "None?"

"You sound uncertain."

"None," Arkh declared.

"That is correct."

"So... Master, am I to understand that I must learn to never make mistakes?"

The Guild Master shook his head. "The ways of humans diverge greatly from the ways of the gods. That is a fact of life. We cannot overcome it. Those who try will spend their lives accomplishing nothing, for no human act can be perfect."

Arkh took many deep breaths. "Master, I'm sorry. I don't understand the lesson."

The Guild Master nodded, smiling, and left Arkh's workbench.

Arkh, gulped, grabbed up the purse with his salary, stuffed it into his cabinet drawer, and returned to his work.

After Arkh finished his design, the Guild Master gave him fishing boat design documents to review. At first, Arkh worried that this was some form of punishment, but then the Guild Master added, "When Methís gets in, we're going down to the docks."

Once the Guild Master had left his workbench, Arkh

released his held in breath and reviewed the designs. It was not Arkh's mistakes that had irritated the Guild Master, but Methís's tardiness. As for the fishing boats, perhaps the council had commissioned a new trawler design.

Arkh tried to focus on the design schematics, but there wasn't much to look at. Fishing boats were rather simple. Sure, there were some complexities around the hooks for the nets. Getting them to fan out appropriately was a fun challenge. But there was no need for fortification against damage, and not much need for human comfort, either.

Now that he looked at it though, he wondered if it would be possible to increase carrying capacity without compromising ballast. Perhaps a wider base—

"Sorry I'm late," Methís called from the door.

"Don't take off your sandals," the Guild Master replied. "We're heading to the docks." He motioned to Arkh.

Arkh jumped off his stool and began putting away his tools. Ilik began putting away his things as well.

After they'd secured the guild, the group of them began down the main road into town. The four of them remained uncomfortably silent. Arkh knew what had delayed Methís, and he wondered how long the situation would continue before the Guild Master had to do something about it. Perhaps he already was, hence the silence. Arkh wondered also if the shipbuilders at the dock were expecting them. Perhaps his group would be noticeably late.

They passed into the city proper, moving past Arkh's house, then beyond to the large stone archway reaching up over the road, its facades adorned with carvings and embellishments of the island's most renowned artists from centuries past. Anatix had made Arkh memorize their names, but Arkh had forgotten nearly all of them.

The streets grew busier as farmers joined merchants and craftsmen in the thoroughfares. Stalls began to line the roads, each little wooden table filled with food and housewares and artwork, everything from paintings to stone figurines.

The air grew saltier, and their street descended toward the beach. Sea breeze blew Arkh's hair up in gusts and the sun shone down warmly.

The dock appeared, row after row of ships, all lined up against wooden platforms built out over the water. Arkh spotted one in particular, a fishing ship which had been suspended in the air by an enormous construct of log supports and rope pulleys.

It had been lifted recently. Beads of water still dropped from its hull, falling and splashing into the sea below.

The Guild Master greeted the Dock Master, and the rest of them stayed silent, as per protocol. Once that formality had been completed, the Guild Master led them out onto the platform and they began their inspection of the ship.

This particular dock consisted of two platforms on either side of the suspended vessel, so that they could analyze both sides.

Arkh diverged from the group, taking the port side of the trawler while the Guild Master, Ilik and Methís took starboard. Arkh immediately began composing a mental list: there were places were the wax and resin had worn away near the front of the hull; barnacles had done permanent damage to the sides; the arms that held the nets out were beginning to fracture—too much stress; and on and on.

He joined up with his coworkers and compared notes. They had noticed the same things on both sides.

"We'll focus on improving the arms that support the nets," the Guild Master said. "The council's mandate is more stable design that requires less maintenance. Those arms have required repair three times in the last seven months."

They discussed the possibilities for many minutes, but Arkh found his mind drifting away from the discussion. Thoughts of Épanngel filled his head.

'Does the Épanngel Shipwright's Guild work on fishing trawlers?' he wondered. He hadn't seen any such designs during his visit. Perhaps they only concerned themselves with bigger, grander ships, like the warship specs tacked up upon their walls. 'They must live on the cutting edge of ship design,' he figured.

"What do you think?" the Guild Master asked Arkh.

Arkh blinked a few times and held his mouth shut.

"I agree," Arkh said, figuring it was the safest thing he could say.

The Guild Master's gaze turned a touch harsh, but he said nothing, merely returned to the topic of his conversation with Ilik and Methís. Arkh paid more attention to the group's discussion after that.

They got lunch afterward at a small cafeteria in the center of the city, then returned to the guild for the rest of the day.

Arkh stayed late, as usual. When his stomach started growling, he raided his desk for his stash of dried beef. Soon, the sky began its shift through the hues, and Arkh reluctantly put away his tools and closed up the guild.

He ran out down the main road in the waning light, away from the city, but not up the mountain. He took the fork that followed the coast instead, running away further down the road as it got rockier and narrower.

And of course, just as the road seemed to disappear altogether into random grass and stones, a small hut appeared, just barely inland from the sandy beach. The glow of candles radiated from the hut's windows and smoke rose from both the fire in the front yard and the chimney of the hut.

Anatix sat outside, tending the fire in his front yard. He was the only person Arkh knew who could tend two fires at once without burning down his house or setting his lawn ablaze.

Anatix looked up and smiled.

Arkh smiled and greeted him by placing both his forearms together before his chest as he approached. Anatix returned the gesture and motioned for Arkh to sit beside him at the fire.

"How have you been?" Anatix said.

"I went to Épanngel, but I bet you already heard about that."

Anatix nodded. "I did. How did you like the big city?"

Arkh bit his lip. Thoughts roiled within his head. "I liked the Guild. Everyone I met there was super sharp and their guild hall was amazing. It's got multiple rooms and two floors, and our tools are crummy compared to theirs. They had whole walls of different designs, some on sheets of paper as tall as I am."

"Sounds very exciting."

"It is." Arkh realized his tone had fallen. He didn't sound excited.

"Well?" Anatix prodded.

Arkh sighed. "Épanngel... freaked me out."

After many moments, Arkh turned and realized Anatix was staring at him, waiting for him to continue.

"Well," Arkh tried again. "The roads are just packed. I thought our streets were busy at midday. In Épanngel, I had to push through people to get anywhere, and I was constantly being bumped into and no one said 'sorry' or 'excuse me' like they do here. And the buildings were enormous. And... there was a way... that I think people were looking at me. I didn't like it. I felt stupid and pathetic, like I'm just some backward hick pretending to be smart and scholarly like them. I don't know. Maybe this whole thing is a dumb idea."

They sat in silence, while the light of the fire danced over them, growing brighter with every moment as the sunlight waned. Stathro sat just above the eastern mountains, her soft, blue light growing brighter as well. Tonight, she was alone.

"Do you remember the ancient story of the moons?" Anatix said, finally.

"Sure," Arkh said.

"Tell it."

"Um, really? I mean I won't do it as good as the bards." Arkh chuckled and shifted his weight.

Anatix retured a resolute glare.

"Okay, sure," Arkh said. "Here goes.

"So, in the beginning, before the earth, there was just nothing—perpetual, empty blackness everywhere. Gods made of pure light moved about it, and each of them held incredible power. Many of them would try to fill the void with their creations, but they fought and quarreled endlessly over what final shape the cosmos should take, and nothing that was created would last for very long because each god was more interested in stopping others from making 'wrong' things than they were in creating things themselves. They spent an eternity thwarting each other and tearing apart one another's creations.

"One day, a god named Isórrop noticed that two other light gods, Atax and Stathro, held a particular interest in tearing apart each other's creations. They didn't go after any other light gods, and other light gods were ignoring them.

"'Why are you constantly bickering only with each other?' Isórrop asked.

"'She destroyed my land!' Atax said.

"'He destroyed my water!' Stathro shot back.

"Isórrop grew intrigued with the concepts of 'land' and 'water.' Even after Atax and Stathro attacked him and destroyed his seeing-hearing-feeling creatures many times over, Isórrop wondered if his creations might not enjoy living on land and water both.

"Isórrop decided not to attack them. He would continue making his seeing-hearing-feeling things over and over, but he would not retaliate.

"'He's not attacking us,' Atax said to Stathro.

"'It's some kind of cruel trick,' Stathro agreed.

"They decided to reverse the trick by stealing his creatures instead of destroying them and interrogating them to learn Isórrop's secrets. One day, when Isórrop was busy defending his creations from others, Atax and Stathro took a herd of goats and some cows and some insects and placed them in a realm of land and water.

"Atax and Stathro reveled in their trickery and watched the creatures they'd stolen, but the more they watched, the more spellbound they grew. Isórrop's creatures had grown and multiplied and changed within the realm of land and water. And they continued to do so.

"'What is the matter?' Isórrop came to them and asked. 'Why have you not attacked me for some time?'

"They pointed to the realm of land and water and Isórrop's creatures, and Isórrop too was spellbound. From that time onward, the three of them agreed to guard the realm of land and water and creatures. And we can see them every night. One or more of them guard us from above, except once every eighteen days, when all of them must rest and none of them appear in our sky. That is a dangerous time, when perhaps other powerful creatures of light may come and wipe the earth away in spite of what Isórrop, Atax, and Stathro have achieved."

Anatix smiled and nodded. It had grown dark, save for Stathro's light, and the light of the fire put Anatix's wrinkled skin into relief. Arkh was accustomed to thinking of Anatix as a young man, someone who would go on forever. He suddenly seemed much less immortal.

"What is the moral behind the myth?" Anatix asked.

"Um..." Arkh sighed and ran it all through his mind again. "I guess it's about how we should create things rather than destroy them."

Anatix nodded. "How do you think Atax and

Stathro felt when they initially hatched their plan?"

Arkh thought it over. "I'm not sure. I'm used to thinking of them as gods, not people."

"Imagine them as people. What would they feel on the eve of stealing Isórrop's creatures?"

"Probably... fear. Fear that Isórrop might retaliate. That something terrible would happen to them. That it was some kind of ingenious counter-counter-trick to lure them away from their creations or expose some other weakness."

"Fear can kill creativity, and ingenuity, too, if you let it," Anatix said. "I taught you how to fly. Do not do me the dishonor of clipping your own wings on the verge of a great adventure just because you are afraid."

Arkh could not help but break a smile. "My biggest worry is really that Épanngel won't want me."

"Neither would that be the end of the world," Anatix shot him a wry smile. "How many cities have governing councils in Palípoli?"

Arkh rolled his eyes and grinned widely. Such a simple question could not be answered without sarcasm. "Four hundred, Master."

Anatix shot him an incredulous, jovial glare.

Arkh threw up his hands. "All right, all right. Eleven."

"You live in Khatap, which is one. Épanngel makes two. What is eleven minus two?"

"Four hundred!"

Anatix laughed. "My point is, even if Épanngel says 'no,' which I highly doubt they will, you have many other options."

They sat and talked for many hours afterward. Anatix told Arkh all about his current students and his challenges with the council. He wished deeply for some kind of guild for instructors and educators, but the council was soundly against it. Still, he pushed and he tried... and he worried about the intentions of some individuals who were vehemently opposed to his ideas.

Eventually, Arkh said goodbye. He did have one more day of work before Féngday, after all. He stood up from the fire and turned away.

"Arkh?" Anatix said.

Arkh turned back to his former teacher. "Yeah?"

"Be... patient with the Guild Master in the coming weeks, okay?"

Arkh wasn't certain what that meant. "Sure," he replied.

As he jogged home under the dim blue glow of the Stathro, Arkh wondered what his future might bring. Épanngel or somewhere else—who knew?

In the meantime, he had a fishing trawler to design. And, he decided, it would be the best damn fishing trawler Khatap had ever seen.

The day after Arkh visited Anatix, he began a routine he would keep for over a week. He woke up early, before even sunrise, and bathed when it was still bitterly windy outdoors. He would then grab food from the kitchen or pantry (usually the pantry, as the service was still busy in the kitchen) and run out the door to work.

He dove head first into the new trawler design, and came up only for food, sleep, and one other ritual. At the end of the day, after the other shipwrights had gone home, Fíl would show up and they would go running.

At the peak of the mountain, Fíl would talk about Merchant's Guild politics and Arkh would describe the fishing boat. It became his world. Nothing else mattered but the ship and his friend.

The day after Arkh's visit with Anatix was Amnday, a typical workday, but the day after that was Féngday, a day most people did not work. The stalls in the marketplace would lie empty and government offices would remain shuttered. Even service staff, like those who worked at Arkh's house, were allowed leisure time on Féngday.

Despite the day of rest, Arkh went to work anyway, and sat alone, working on a design for a ship that would be able to support fishing nets that wouldn't have long, easily damaged arms. The problem, he was sure, lay in the immense pressure that caught fish exerted on the material, which the netting itself could cope with, but not the wooden supports that held them. The drag coefficient would only exacerbate the damage. He had either to come up with a way to craft more durable support arms, or find a way to extend the nets without using arms at all.

Fíl showed up at the Shipwright's Guild on the afternoon of that Féngday.

"Man, what are you doing here?" Fíl called out.

"Come see," Arkh said, not looking up from his work.

His desk had become littered with fishing boat designs and schematics for various netting support structures that had been used in the past, either by Khatap or other cities.

"What is all this?" Fíl asked.

"Fishing boats."

"I can see that."

Fíl joined him all the same, and measured and checked the math while Arkh assiduously worked through calculations for length, height, stress, and support strength.

It was only when Fíl yawned that Arkh looked out the window and realized the sun had already set. He grinned and nodded to the door. Fíl sighed and nodded his approval, and the two disrobed and took off running up the mountain.

The next week went by in much the same fashion. By Asterday of the following week, Arkh had formed a potential solution. Ilik looked upon it with a bemused smile. Methís gasped, clearly shocked that an initiate member had contrived such a thing.

Finally, on Chryday, it came time to show the Guild

Master. Arkh had to hold his hands behind his back to keep them from shaking, but he managed to bring the Guild Master to his desk and show him his idea.

"I think," Arkh said, "that we could try lining the edges of the nets with wooden floatation buoys. Then there would be no need for an arm or support. If each end of the rope holding the buoys is attached to one side of the ship, it will fully extend. There will be greater drag, but I didn't think speed would be an issue for a fishing boat."

The Guild Master was silent for many dreadfully tense moments.

He blinked. Then he nodded. Then he nodded again. He opened his mouth. Then he closed it.

White seeped in at the edges of Arkh's vision. If his mouth hadn't been clamped shut, he'd have been hyper-ventilating.

"Not bad," the Guild Master blurted out.

Ilik slapped Arkh on the back and laughed.

No higher praise from the Guild Master could be achieved.

The Guild Master went back about his work and Arkh and Ilik spent the rest of the day talking about the new fishnet design.

The next day was an Amnday, and Arkh followed his usual routine. More excited than ever to continue his work on the trawler, he rushed through bathing and breakfast, ran to work, opened up the guild, got out his supplies, opened the window, and—

A bireme passed by on the sea beyond his window, heading in the direction of Khatap's port. The insignia upon its hull was clear even from the distance: a double bar of red atop waves of blue, the insignia of Épanngel.

Arkh watched it float by until it passed around the hill Khatap sat upon.

Part of him wanted to take off running toward the port, and another part of him wanted to hide in the closet and not come out until the ship had gone.

He pulled out his design schematics for the nets and the new trawler with hooks, riggings and special pulleys to lift the nets out of the water rather than retract them on wooden supports.

But they remained a fuzzy, white, unintelligible splotch upon his workbench.

His mind was stuck on that Épanngelian bireme parked in the harbor. What was their business in Khatap? Did any of it involve him? Was there a letter? A courier? Or were they here for something else? It could still be that another ship would arrive in a couple of days or weeks. Épanngel's Shipwright Guild could get back to him whenever they chose to, including never if that was what they decided.

His coworkers filtered into the guild, and he knew he should work, but he could not shake away his daze.

"Something wrong?" Methís asked him at lunch hour.

"No, nothing," Arkh said.

Ilik was grinning widely as he ate the sandwich he'd brought from home, and Methís noticed. "What do you know?"

"I saw an Épanngel bireme sail into port this morning while I was in the market."

Realization dawned on Methís's face. "You should go home. They'll probably take the letter there."

Arkh shook his head vigorously back and forth. The last thing he wanted was to be stuck around his parents all day.

But as lunchtime passed, he found all the equations and formulae that had so captivated him the last week had become desiccated hunks of boredom and despair. He could not concentrate on them to save his life. He found himself staring at the sea, and only realizing he'd been doing so after minutes had passed.

"Arkh." The Guild Master had appeared in front of his workbench.

Arkh jumped, grabbed up his pencil and adjusted himself on his stool. "Yes, Master?"

"Go home."

"No, really, Master, I'm—"

"Go home, Arkh. You must come back here when the courier has arrived, and you will tell us all what is in your letter."

Arkh's mouth moved up and down a few times, but his voice box produced no sound.

"Arkh?" the Guild Master said.

"Yes?"

"Go home."

"Yes, Master."

Arkh nodded, slowly stored away his tools, slid his stool underneath his desk, moved to the door, wrapped up his feet, and proceeded out away from the guild. He began down the main road at a walk, but the further he went, the faster he walked, until he broke into a jog, then a run.

He arrived back at home, came to the door and saw no letter or notice of any kind.

He opened the door, entered, closed it gently behind him.

"Who's there?" his father's voice.

Arkh winced. "It's just me, sir."

"Arkh?"

"Yes, sir."

"Come in here."

Arkh walked into his father's study, which was the second right off the main foyer, just beyond the front door. Arkh walked in, slowly. Paintings lined the walls. His father had even commissioned a statue of his favorite god, which stood in the corner. He sat at his desk, scrawling on parchment. Even at his age, with graying hair, he still managed to seem imposing. Arkh constantly had to remind himself that he was adult now, too. His father always managed to make him feel like a child.

"Why are you home from work so early?"

"The Guild Master sent me home, sir."

"Was there some problem with your work?"

"No, sir. Not that I know of."

"You should find out. You have been working hard recently. Perhaps a bit too hard. Don't overdo it. That lad who studied with you under your mentor... the one who works for the Merchant's Guild..."

"I think you mean Fíl, sir."

"Right, Fíl. I knew his father. Good man. Very unfortunate. Part of that was him working too hard, you know. Put in too many long days, and the work he was in... Well, he should have taken better care of his health is all."

"Yes, sir. I'll be careful."

"Good boy. Now, about your friends sending you messages via courier."

Arkh's eyes jolted wide open and he stood rigid at a board.

His father didn't seem to notice. "The one who arrived today mispronounced our family name horribly. At first I thought he was just dull, but I looked at his envelope, and whoever had written it had spelled our family name with two O's instead of one, and a C instead of a K-H. Now, if you're going to receive post at this house, that's fine, but I must insist that you tell whoever it is you're corresponding with to spell our family name correctly."

"Sir, may I ask…?"

"You may."

"What happened to the courier?"

"I sent him away, of course."

Emotions surged within Arkh—rage and contempt foremost among them. But Arkh knew how to handle his father. He'd had twenty years of experience, after all.

"Sir," Arkh said, keeping his tone as level as he could, "I would like your permission to leave the household for a trip into the city."

"Is this letter important?"

"Yes, sir."

"Well, please make sure that whoever it is learns proper spelling."

"Yes, sir. I will, sir."

"Good boy."

It took all of Arkh's willpower not to bolt out the door of his father's study. He stood, silently fuming, willing his father to speak the necessary words.

"You may go," his father finally added.

Arkh walked carefully to the door, pulled it carefully open, shut it carefully, walked to the front door, wrapped his feet, his movements growing ever faster, he pulled open the front door, shut it very carefully and precisely so as not to make any extra noise, jogged down the path to the main street, opened the gate, closed the gate, latched it—

And took off into a sprint.

He had never run so fast in all his life. By the time he reached the stone archway, he was maneuvering and dodging other passersby. By the time he reached the market he was ducking and weaving amongst the crowd.

"Sorry!"

"Excuse me!"

"Pardon!"

He became an endless, running, weaving, panting, human ball of shouted apologies. He hurtled down the hill, and to his great relief, the Épanngel bireme was still docked in the harbor.

"Wait!" Arkh shouted as he careened down the hill. "Don't leave!"

He hurtled onto the dock, the Dock Master trailing behind him shouting complaints, but Arkh surged ahead to where two men in Épanngelian dress stood talking before a plank of wood leading from the dock into the ship.

"I'm so sorry, excuse me but—" Arkh started.

"What do you think you're doing?" The Dock Master roared.

Arkh turned to him. "I'm so sorry, but my father didn't take my letter for me, and I had to get them before they left."

"Are you Arkh Makhaino?" one of the Épanngelians said, a tall man with a scraggly blond beard. His Épanngelian accent was thick with rounded vowels and lightened consonants.

"Yes," Arkh said. "That's me."

"Go get Tacíd," the Épanngelian said to his companion, who promptly walked up the plank and disappeared into his ship.

Arkh was then forced to turn his attention back to the Dock Master, where he absorbed a lecture about proper procedure for the dock, and its importance, because docks could be dangerous places, and so many valuable goods passed through here, and security was of the utmost importance, because people expected their cargo and belongings to remain safe, and blah, blah, blah.

Arkh apologized until he was blue in the face.

Another blond Épanngelian man emerged from the bireme alongside the one who'd left.

"Arkh Makhaino?"

"Yes?"

"This is for you."

The man handed over a large envelope of green-dyed paper, with his name inscribed, albeit misspelled, upon it. A seal of cream colored wax adorned the lip of the envelope.

Arkh's hands trembled. He could not open it. He didn't know how.

"Well," the Dock Master said, "you ran all the way here and broke into my dock to get that thing. You better open it."

Arkh gulped and pulled at the wax seal. The lid of the envelope popped open, and Arkh peered inside.

There were multiple documents, but one in particular had a ribbon on it, and the paper was embroidered with some kind of clothy material.

Arkh pulled it out and read:

Dear Arc Macainoo:

The Shipwright's Guild of Épanngel hereby requests your employ in the service of ship design and engineering. You will receive the rank of novice and perform duties within our guild under the auspices of the Épanngel City Council. You shall receive a weekly stipend of fifty-eight kermáta for your services.

Please send the enclosed reply envelope back at your earliest convenience with a response of either "accept" or "decline." We hope you choose to accept this position, and if so, we look forward to seeing you soon.

You will find enclosed all documents you will require to safely enter Épanngel port. If you send along your travel itinerary and the itinerary of your ship of passage, we can have someone meet you on the dock on the day of your arrival.

Sincerely,
Diethi Thetis, Shipwright Guild Master
Épanngel Port City

Arkh ran his eyes over the first sentence many times, just to be sure it said what he thought it said.

"Well?" the Dock Master asked. Though he stood right beside Arkh, his voice sounded dozens of mettrs distant.

Arkh turned his face up to the sky, leapt, punched the air, and shouted 'yes' at the top of his lungs.

Arkh begged the Dock Master to loan him a pencil until the Dock Master finally acquiesced. Arkh drew a broad circle around the word 'accept' upon the acceptance document, stashed it inside the enclosed envelope, and then begged the Dock Master to help him seal it.

The Dock Master's show of annoyance concealed his vicarious joy. Khatap citizens getting jobs on the mainland were a times of celebration—the community enjoyed recognition that powerful mainland cities held their citizens in high enough regard to snipe them away, even though few mainlanders found their way to Khatap's shores as anything but visitors.

Arkh hurried the response envelope into the hands of Épanngelians at the dock, who turned out to be the ship's captain. He accepted with a wide, knowing smile.

"Shipwright's Guild, eh? Congratulations. You know, I'll be back here in two weeks' time for another supply run. If that's not too late, you could come on board my ship if you'd like. Our crew quarters aren't fancy, mind you."

Arkh was nodding vigorously up and down before the captain had finished relating his offer.

"I'll be sure to tell them when to expect you." The captain winked.

"Thank you!" Arkh beamed, and performed the gesture of respect with his forearms pressed together before his chest. The captain returned the gesture.

"My ship is called the Akver Psíc."

"I'll be here and ready to go when you arrive, Captain Akver," Arkh replied.

They talked for some time more, the Dock Master promising to let him into the harbor in two weeks' time only if Arkh promised to follow proper entry procedure. The captain laughed, but Arkh insistently promised to follow every one of the Dock Master's rules to the letter.

Arkh said his farewell to Captain Akver and left the docks, meandering up the hill in a daze, clasping his green envelope. His fellow citizens passed by him in a blur. His entire world seemed draped in a surreal shroud—in sixteen short days, he would leave Khatap, not forever, but certainly he would not be returning often or for very long.

He would be making his life in Épanngel, the third largest Palípolian city. It possessed the second most powerful military, too, a fact they liked to tout over Meigá. He would work on ships in one of the most powerful navies in the known world. He felt maybe he should pinch himself to see if he were dreaming.

When he reached the marketplace, details of his surroundings began to flit into his attention. Many of the merchants were closing down their stalls and the sun was low in the sky. It occurred to him that his coworkers were waiting for him back at the guild. The Guild Master had instructed him to bring his news back to them.

And so, though his legs were still sore from his earlier sprint, Arkh burst into yet another run, away from the marketplace, under the arch, past his home, until he came, panting and sweating, to the door of the Shipwright's Guild.

The Guild Master stood at the front door, his arms folded. "Well?"

Panting so hard he was unable to speak, Arkh handed over the envelope, which had grown wrinkled from being clenched so hard and had absorbed no small amount of Arkh's sweat. But the Guild Master took it all the same, pulled out the acceptance letter, scanned his eyes over it, and smiled.

Even through exhaustion, Arkh noticed something else. The Guild Master's eyes were—at first he thought disappointed, but that was not quite it either. He was sad. All at once, Anatix's request from that night over a week ago came back to him. The Guild Master did not begrudge him leaving—he was sad to see him go.

"Good job, Arkh," the Guild Master said.

"Thank you, Master."

"Did he get it?" Ilik appeared at the door, with Methís close behind him.

The Guild Master handed over the envelope and Methís opened it while Ilik looked over his shoulder.

"Way to go, Arkh," Ilik said.

Arkh beamed and time seemed to pass into a blur once more. The Guild Master took the four of them out to dinner at Khatap's fanciest restaurant. He ordered them a bottle of wine that had been imported from Piirka-Í, and they ate goat stewed in a mushroom cream sauce. Arkh went home slightly tipsy and with the vague notion of congratulations and well wishes from his colleagues.

When he rolled out of bed the next morning, even groggier than usual, he began to think through his usual routine, including the nets on the fishing trawler, until his eyes landed upon the green envelope on his night-stand.

The events of the previous day came rolling back at him, crashing over him like a breaking wave.

He remembered something else—the date. Today was Khorday, a special designation for the first Féngday of every month. On normal Féngdays, guild workers, government officials, and other skilled workers would rest, while service staff and manual laborers, like the ones on his family's property, would remain obligated to some relatively trivial tasks.

On Khorday, or Kens, as most people called it, work and production ceased utterly.

Nothing was harvested, nothing was planted, nothing was traded, nothing of any import was done at all.

Tonight was the night that the sky would remain black and dead even without cloud cover. Tonight was the night that not one of their three moons would shine.

Arkh puttered about his room, going downstairs only for food and water. He did not talk to his parents, or anyone else. Khorday was not for making or contriving anything. No interactions on a Khorday could come of any good, and his family and fellow citizens would feel the same way.

He read story scrolls on Khordays, usually, but today, he found himself going over the contents of his envelope over and over again, thinking through the itinerary in his mind, but he didn't dare write anything down. He wouldn't jinx his great fortune by committing any plans on a Khorday. And yet, he couldn't wait for Captain Akver to return.

Arkh found his mind also straying to his parents. His anger at their behavior, these last ten years especially, grew the more he pondered them. All of his father's arrogance and his mother's selfishness. He would tell them the next morning. He would really tell them. And then he would leave. And good riddance, too!

He went to sleep that night thinking it through, and how glad he would be to do it. He would march off to his new job as a free man.

Arkh woke up fresh the next morning, the thoughts of the previous night still ripe in his mind. He did not rush off to work early. Instead, he bathed and dressed leisurely, and made a point of taking his breakfast with his family. He grinned the entire time as he absently washed himself. He played the exact conversation through in his mind—what he would say, what they would say, what he would say in response. And finally, he would tell them what he really thought of them, about how he was going to go to Épanngel and make something of the family name that others would look upon with reverence instead of contempt.

He carried the envelope with him down to breakfast.

"Good morning, Arkh!" his mother said, already sitting at the dining room table. "Why, I don't think I've seen you in over a week. What have you been up to?"

"Just working hard," Arkh said.

"Good boy," his father said between bites of oatmeal. "Just remember what I said yesterday. Don't overdo it. I'm glad you joined us for breakfast today. I see you got your envelope. What's inside?"

Arkh found his indignation settling into something he found vaguely disgusting. Was that the lesson he would take from them? That he should return their foibles with callousness and capriciousness, especially as he sat under their roof and ate their food? He felt real shame, just then.

"It's a letter, sir. From Épanngel."

"Oh!" His mother brought her hands up to her face and covered her mouth. "Then... the Shipwright's Guild—?"

Arkh smiled and nodded.

His father stood from his seat, his eyes wide.

Arkh stood slowly from his chair.

His father walked around the table, put one hand on Arkh's shoulder, then, his face seeming to melt, he pulled his son closer into a hug.

Arkh stiffened. Startled. His father had never hugged him in all his life.

His father released him and clapped him on the shoulder. The look in his eyes was hard to read. Pride, Arkh thought. Genuine pride. Shame at his earlier thoughts washed over him anew.

His father nodded, sat down once again, and resumed eating his oatmeal.

Arkh sat down as well.

"We will send you off with some money. I know that the guild probably said that they'd float you a loan for your first month, but I want them to know that we Khatapans can work as hard as the rest of them."

"Sir, I'm sure that that's really not necessary—"

"I insist," he said. "And you'll write to your mother

regularly, too."

"Yes, sir."

"Oh," his mother released her hands from her face, her eyes streaming tears. "I'll need to make you some nice robes for when you go out, and you'll need a proper pair of sandals, and what about the boat, dear?" She turned to his father. "We don't want him eating that fermented, salted tack all the way to Épanngel, do we?"

"The boat food's really not that bad," Arkh said. Every passing moment seemed to increase his guilt over his attitude the previous day. No good could come of plans made upon a Khorday, he reminded himself.

In the end, he slunk out of the dining hall wondering how he'd feel about leaving his family after all. His father seemed to have words for everything except the most important matters. Arkh had seen how mixed his emotions had been at breakfast—he'd felt sorry that he'd sent the courier away, he'd just been too stubborn to admit it. And the pride he'd felt at Arkh's accomplishment had seemed utterly genuine.

He would write them every week, he decided, on Féngday, and to both of them, too.

When he arrived at the guild, he found he could finally concentrate upon his work. He also found that his relationship to the other guildsmen, even the Guild Master, had subtly changed. He was no longer the kid under tutelage. They treated him more like a mini-Guild Master, and he found the experience strange. He had only received a green envelope. It was no magic talisman or symbol from the gods.

He was still just a twenty-year-old guy. He had all the same knowledge and abilities that he'd had the day before.

Arkh stayed late at work, well after the others had left. The light of the sun grew dim, barely glowing from behind the mountains, and sky above the port had already turned black. The faint twinkle of stars appeared.

He sighed and put away his things, stowed away his stool, and had nearly reached the door when it swung inward, causing him to catch his breath.

Fíl strode in the door, nearly bumping into him.

"Oh, sorry," Fíl said.

"No problem," Arkh replied. "So, you'll never believe—"

"How about a run?"

"Sure, but—"

"Let's go."

Fíl tossed off his robe, letting it fall to the floor by the door, then ran out to the intersection where the guild's small road met the main road.

Arkh furrowed his brow, wondering what was the matter with Fíl while he wrapped up his feet and disrobed. He jogged out and joined his friend, and merely took up his starting pose, deciding not to push the subject of his acceptance again until Fíl had gotten their run.

Fíl won their race, of course.

They sat at the mountain peak, looking down on their city, glowing tonight under Isórrop's bright, white glow.

Fíl sat down beside him. "When do you leave?"

Arkh blinked a few times, wondering who had told him. Probably a merchant knew a dock worker, the usual way word got around.

"Two weeks from Thálday, assuming my ship's not delayed."

"I hear there are pirates out there, you know."

"And a guy could fall of a cliff, too."

"That's not funny."

"I wasn't trying to be."

Silence.

"Look, Fíl—"

"I want to run. Every day. Even on Féngdays."

"Sure."

"Even if it rains."

"Okay."

"Even if there's sleet."

"Have you even seen sleet? I know I haven't."

"I'm just sayin', I don't want there to be any excuses."

"Remember when we saw that water spout though?"

Fíl smiled. "Yah. That was pretty wicked."

They sat and talked for an hour or more. Arkh did not attempt to bring up the subject of Épanngel, and all of Fíl's topics of conversation remained centered on

Khatap. Arkh ran home that night wondering about all the strange variations on his life the day had brought him.

And so the days went on much as they had before, albeit in this new, slightly altered form. His parents were the most attentive and caring they had ever been in his entire memory of life in his home. His mother still gossiped up a storm and made a point of bragging about him at every turn, and his father still refused to ask him anything about his life. However, his mother did supply him with food and clothes and scrolls and luggage of all sorts at every turn, while his father brought home information and records from the city council halls, everything he could get his hands on that Khatap officials knew about the political workings of Épanngel.

Arkh never would have guessed that their love for him might manifest itself in such ways, though their old attitudes and behaviors remained essentially unchanged.

Work remained work, although he still felt his interactions there odd and unfamiliar. Though the newfound respect felt unearned and unjustified, he accepted it with all the grace and dignity he could manage.

He and Fíl ran every night. One night it drizzled, and another night it poured, and yet they ran all the same. On the night of the downpour, they found shelter underneath the trees and made themselves a fire. They talked of work, mostly. Fíl occasionally mentioned a girl he'd been seeing on and off for the last few weeks.

"Is it serious?" Arkh asked.

Fíl shrugged.

Two weeks passed in that manner, until Arkh found he'd arrived at the Asterday prior to the day of his departure. With a deep sigh and much inner turmoil, he spent the day rolling up his completed trawler designs into large scrolls, then he cleared out his desk, moved his toolkit to the commons area of the guild, set his stool aside, looked over his desk, and all at once, he realized it was not his anymore.

He walked to the Guild Master's office and knocked.

"Master?"

"Yes, Arkh."

"I— I'm leaving for Épanngel tomorrow."

The Guild Master nodded with a frown, his eyes making a good attempt at contacting Arkh's but not quite achieving it. He stood from his chair, and placed his forearms together in front his chest.

Arkh returned the gesture.

"Safe journey," the Guild Master said.

"Thank you, Master."

"You may call me Daskl."

"I—" Arkh's mouth hung open for many moments. He gulped. "I'm not sure I could ever get used to that."

"You will."

"Hey." Ilik appeared at his side, clapped him on the shoulder and pushed a wooden box into Arkh's chest. "Methís and I got you this."

"What is—?" Arkh took and pulled open the lid. Inside lay a compass of the finest metal, inscribed with Arkh's full name. A set of pencils, too, all carved of pure elm wood, even a small sharpener block with a razor. The bottom of the box was lined with blue cotton. And then Arkh saw—his name was inscribed in the base of the box, too.

"Oh my gods," Arkh muttered. "I can't accept this. It must have cost a fortune!"

"You'll accept it all right." Methís appeared at his other side.

Arkh had not been a hugger, but he hugged them both regardless, and did not hold back tears either.

And in that moment, he realized his deep inner turmoil at leaving Khatap. This was no longer an island he wanted to discard like a beat-up cloak. This was home. Khatap Island was special.

He and Fíl ran that night. He'd found Arkh at his home. It was the first and only time he'd come to Arkh's home.

And so they ran, this time not to the mountain top, but to Anatix's hut instead. He sat, as usual, around the fire burning brightly in his front yard. Cloud cover hid the glow of the moons, and waves thrashed against the nearby shore.

"You all ready to go?" Anatix said as they sat down beside him.

"Well," Arkh said, "I've got all the stuff I need. I

wouldn't say I'm ready though."

Fíl and Anatix shared a knowing look.

Fíl looked at him. "You're going to have a great time, Arkh. I'd be lying if I said I wasn't jealous."

"And I'd be lying if I said I didn't want to stay," Arkh mumbled at the fire.

"All of your life is here," Anatix said. "And that makes leaving hard, especially with so many invested in your success. But remember why you went after this job. This island has limits that minds like yours aren't meant to be constrained by."

"Oh, come on." Arkh threw up his hands. "I'm sick of that, too—everyone treating me like I'm some kind of prodigy. I'm just a guy."

"A guy with a good brain and a good heart to boot," Fíl said. "You realize how rare that combination is in the world? You think I stuck with you as a friend because I thought I couldn't do any better? Well I have news for you."

Anatix poked at his fire. "You two share those qualities."

The trio remained silent. No one wanted to take that discussion any farther, for it might lead to the topic of why Fíl would remain on Khatap for the foreseeable future.

"You are the finest two students I have ever had," Anatix said.

"Thank you," Arkh and Fíl both replied.

"For everything you've taught us," Fíl added.

"Have you learned much about Épanngel these last few days?" Anatix asked.

"Yeah." Arkh relaxed his posture. "Dad's been bringing stuff home for me to read."

"Tell me about it," Anatix said with a grin. "I've been dying to know what secrets the council keeps hidden from us lowly educators."

Arkh told him everything he knew and more, details gleaned from his three-day adventure prior that had gained new meaning in the context of what he'd learned from the scrolls his father had brought home.

The clouds cleared, and Atax joined them, a ruddy, maroon glow bathing everything in sight. The red suffused Arkh and Fíl's run back to Arkh's house. Arkh thought back to the old stories for Atax's nights, which occurred after the fourteenth and fifteenth day of every month, the only two nights when Atax ruled the sky alone: 'Katkási, the time of chaos.'

Chaos indeed. Arkh was uprooting his entire life and hurling it across eighty thousand mettrs of the Messig.

To the mainland.

His feet pounded across the dirt, and sweat dripped down his chest and his arms and his legs. It was a warm night for Early Autumn.

They stopped at the gates to Arkh's house, where Fíl took his golden robes from off the fencepost where he'd hung them.

"Hey, Arkh."

"Yeah?"

"Take care in the big city."

"More than anyone else on Khatap, I wish you could come with me."

"It's not my adventure, man." Fíl squeezed his shoulder. "It's yours."

"You take care of yourself, too." Arkh said. "Okay?"

Fíl nodded. "I will." Then he turned and walked away toward the city, not looking back into the night. Arkh stood and watched him go, until his friend had gone farther than he could see.

He trudged slowly into his home, threw himself onto his bed, and fell instantly to sleep.

The next morning, he grabbed up his pack—a piece of cloth wrapping up food and clothes and the box that his colleagues had given him—and, wearing his navy blue Shipwright's robes, he descended from his room, hugged his parents goodbye, walked away from his house, and down to the harbor.

He waited only two hours, staring out across the sea with the wind tussling his hair one way and then the other, before the Épanngelian ship Akver Psíc drifted into view on the horizon.

PERSISTENCE, VISION, FOCUS

...won't be able to handle it...
...mind's a mess...
...better off running the Feros Road...

Silence.

...failure...
...not really good at anything...
...gotta do something useful, might as well mine ore like other grunts...

Silence.

Estí grew aware of the beads of sweat upon his brow, of the twitching of his eyebrow, of the fidget working its way through his right big toe. He tried to push the awareness away, but it blossomed and expanded through his consciousness.

And there he was.

Waves of heat seared up off the ground, and a vulture shrieked somewhere above him. A wolf skull lay in the sand, shimmering, some ten mettrs beyond where he sat.

Estí grunted and grabbed up his skein. He drank carefully and meagerly, giving himself only just enough so that he might regain some feeling in his tongue. He wiped at his brow and flicked the sweat away.

'Why do you fight this, Estí?' Even his mentor had been against him. 'Your grandfather was a Feros Runner, and your father, too. What do you hope to accomplish with this?'

'I wish to see what the samánii describe.'

His teacher had sighed and frowned, rumpling his brow like beaten pillow. 'The samánii are very gifted.'

Those five words had hurt Estí more deeply than any of the taunts of his peers or the exasperated expression of his withered father.

'Why am I out here?' he asked himself for what seemed like the millionth time. He moved his mouth without speaking the words aloud, though they reverberated through his mental world, echoing again and again and again inside his skull.

He and Nomio had gone out into the desert many times before, and Estí would sit and watch how his friend would sit, silently, and the heat would bake them both, though they wore their people's wide cloth hats to protect their head and torsos, and the light slacks and foot wrappings to protect the rest from the sun's harsh gaze.

Nearer to Piirka-Í, the desert contained cacti and other signs of vegetation that the occasional rainstorm allowed. Here the plateau went on for mettrs and mettrs and it was all dead and flat and gritty, everything shimmering off-yellow orange, and the sky was a lighter shade of blue, almost grey-white.

Once, Nomio's eyes had flitted open. Estí had dropped his gaze to the ground, ashamed.

'No?' Nomio had asked.

Estí had shaken his head.

'Let's try again.' Nomio had suggested.

'Sun's almost down.' Estí had begun tracing circles in the sand with his finger. 'I'll try again next time.'

Nomio had reached out and stayed Estí's hand just then. 'Again.'

And Estí had released an exasperated sigh and put his hands back in his lap, and he and Nomio had both sat silently with their eyes closed until nightfall.

A bead of sweat traced its way down his arm, and Estí felt it glide down, ricocheting off arm hair after arm hair until finally it slipped off the edge of his elbow, hurtling into the sand. He had the thought that he should go back to the city and accept his fate. He would take up his father's pickax and put on his old mining clothes, and then he'd join the caravan next Dasday.

The miners worked a monthly cycle—northward on the Feros Road on the second, arrival at the mountains occurred on the fourth, usually, barring bad weather. They would mine at night and camp during the day for eleven days before returning to Piirka-Í for two whole days of rest before their next trip.

The Feros Runners, all of them men, burned up quickly. Their skin turned from brown to black under the scorching power of the sun, and their lungs filled with ash and other toxins from the mines. His father hacked and coughed and lay in bed mostly these days. Estí took care of him as best he could, but without his mother...

He had to push that thought away. His meager skein would barely replenish his body's fluids as it was. He could not afford tears.

His father lay at home now. Estí wondered if his father was uncomfortable, if he had enough water and food. Sometimes Estí couldn't hear him calling, because his father's voice had become so scratchy that Estí could not make it out over the roar of the forge, which he now operated alone. It was a very old thing that burned hotter than it should and was already showing signs of rust and decay. But with Estí running it, they could pay for their house. They could survive.

And Estí could run off into the desert and entertain the notion that he might one day see what the samánii see—the visions his friend Nomio had already caught glimpses of in his mind when he sat in the desert and Atax came out and glowed red chaos down upon Palípoli.

Atax shone alone only on the fourteenth and the fifteenth days of the month. On other nights it was joined by its siblings, Isórrop and Stathro. Today was the fifteenth of the month, and the night, when it came, would be called Katkási, time of chaos. And somewhere, many hundreds of mettrs from here, the Feros Runners were beginning the last leg of their march across the ocean of sand separating the fertile coastal city Piirka-Í from the rich mountains of iron in the north.

His back dripped sweat now, and he realized the sun was behind rather than above him.

Had it really grown so late?

'Time sure is moving quickly,' Estí thought to himself, then realized with a jolt that he had lost track of time. He took a very deep breath in, then a very deep breath out. He thought of—

Silence.

His eyes were closed, but unfathomably complex whorls of color formed in his mind's eye. Time distended and unraveled. The wolf skull appeared before him and mingled with the whorls. An incredible calm suffused him entirely: mind, body and soul.

He sat in this state for what seemed like hours, then opened his eyes to the realization that all was dark and cold and Atax's red light had blasted everything into a violent blood hue. The whole plain of sand was maroon and silent. The vultures had gone; Nothing stirred.

Slowly, Estí drew himself up to a stance. His muscles ached like never before in his life, and his whole body jolted with uncontrollable bouts of shivering. So unbearably cold.

Estí looked up at Atax and smiled. He thought of his father, and of his mentor.

"Thank you," he told the red moon.

No one wouldn't believe him, of course. He'd tell them the truth, and they'd deny him all the same. And really, when he thought about it, he didn't particularly care about membership in the samánii. That was Nomio's path, not his.

He let the tears slide down his face as he downed the rest of his skein. It seemed unreal—he'd achieved his experience. He would have something nice, after all, to take with him on the Feros Road.

SIMPLE REASON

Foit sat and stared at his mentor, not with anger or fear or worry, or any other such negative emotions. He merely thought. Dox, master of the Guild of Reason, sat and stared back, both kindly and patiently.

"What if..." Foit began, then seemed to reconsider his words. The other students, seated in a semi-circle around him, lurched to attention and caught their breath. All attention shifted to Foit.

"What if," Foit nodded as he spoke, "I take a hunk of bark and divide it in half. Then I divide it in half again. Then again, and again, and again. Shall I keep doing so forever?"

The students turned their attention to Dox.

Dox kept his eyes fixed on Foit. "The bark shall grow infinitely smaller by halves, approaching but never becoming nothing."

Back to Foit.

Foit quirked his eyelashes and looked momentarily up at the sky before facing his teacher once more. "But... is tree bark really a fundamental component? I mean, for example, if I churn milk to butter, but then let it rest, the milk and fat separate. Could not bark too eventually divide out into separate components?"

"Ah," Dox said. "But the size at which one would have to cut to make such a separation would be very small. Men cannot hold knives such as you describe."

"Trees grow out of the earth," Foit said. "Perhaps bark shall become earth again if subdivided many times."

"Perhaps." Dox pursed his lips. "Let us return to the question of divisibility. Can we know whether or not we might divide forever? Or might we reach a point at which we can subdivide no further? Lacking knives so tiny we cannot hope to hold them, how can we tell?"

Foit took a deep breath. The other students looked at him with wide eyes, silently cheering him on.

"Well," Foit mumbled. His facial features crumpled in upon themselves. Dox noticed the faint traces of perspiration upon his student's brow, and many moments passed. The tension of the silent students, all willing their compatriot to succeed, grew and grew, bordering on intolerable.

All of a sudden, Foit perked up. "Solid material does not recombine! If I cut a log in half, it is irrevocably cut. If I tear a scroll, it is irrevocably torn. I cannot take those pieces and put them back the way they were before they were hewn."

"And so?" Dox asked with a smirk.

"So, with solid things the division must end. If separations can go on forever and nothing can be recombined, then we would end up with a world where the solid things must all be very, very small. The existence of large solids in our world implies the existence of some minimum size at which the material is still itself and not something else."

"Do not children grow larger as they become adults?"

"Yes..." Foit deflated. "They consume much solid and liquid nutrition. Our bodies must be capable of breaking that material into components so small that they can be absorbed into the rest of us. Perhaps at a smaller level recombination is easier?"

Dox wagged a finger. "You have arrived at speculation."

Foit's face fell. "I'm sorry, master."

"Look up."

The young man did.

"You did very well." Dox then spread out his hands, as he did when he addressed all his students. The assembled students rose to their feet as one. Foit's frown remained.

"Think upon this lesson," Dox said. "We will certainly discuss the materiality of our world in a future lesson. Be ready. Also, I noticed a certain amount of tension and emotion from the group today. Please remember, especially as a participant in a dialogue, that reason and logic cannot function when impeded by emotion. I want everyone to practice calm and collected mental control this evening. Sit and think silently without distraction for at least an hour. Focus on reigning in your emotions, so that your reason might be the tower, which no bombardment can topple."

"Yes, master," the pupils said as one.

"You are dismissed." About half the young men ran away from the grove and off toward the road that led into the city. The other half crowded around Dox, Foit among them. Questions assaulted him from many directions at once.

Dox held up his hands. "I am heading to Ígia to see how the new hall is coming along. You may join me, but only if you take turns asking me your questions."

He took off toward the road, an entourage of students following behind him, each of them anxious to engage him in one line of questioning or another. He maintained a policy of dialogues only during instruction sessions, but students flocked to him after lessons regardless. The Guild of Reason had only four members: three mentors, including himself, and one head master. Only the mentors taught. Dox would have liked to be head master one day, but he suspected he would be too old by the time the current head master resigned. The head master seemed eager to stay in his position as long as he still breathed.

But Dox genuinely enjoyed teaching, and was glad for the daily practice of utilizing logic. He had to admit, he would rather own his problem of an overzealous student body, rather than the problem faced by the Guild of Agriculture or the Guild of Bards: lack of interest. The council was constantly hounding the mentors of those guilds to justify the wages they were paid.

As Dox liked to remind his students, rationalizing the world was the foundation of all other human works. Without reason, there could be no farms, no ships, no tools, nor even an understanding of the gods. Reason underpinned everything.

His entourage fell away until only Foit followed him. Conifers grew thick along the sides of the road, and it rose too, the incline growing steeper every moment.

"What are the ramifications of today's lesson, master?" Foit finally asked.

Dox stopped and put a hand on the student's shoulder. "You are not the first pupil to run into folly upon his first dialogue."

Foit quivered. He nodded, his face toward the ground. "Yes, master."

"Did you come all this way just to ask this question?"

Another nod.

"Put thoughts of expulsion out of your mind. However, you must master these emotions you are laying bare before me if you wish to proceed further with your studies in the Guild of Reason."

"Yes, master." His voice cracked. "May I go home now?"

"No. Your mastery of this undue shame begins now. Come with me."

Foit looked up and blinked a few times. Confusion replaced self-reproach upon his features. Dox turned and continued up the hill.

The two of them strode forward in silence.

The hill leveled out, and a wooden frame came into view. Stumps still littered the ground, surrounding the skeleton of cinched logs at the center. Behind the grove, the ground proceeded up a steep incline. The gentle murmur of falling water signaled the presence of Ígia Falls in the distance. Already, builders had dug a trench which would soon be lined with stones, and into which the river would be diverted so that it led around this property.

This would be The Hall of Reason at Ígia, a location befitting the prestige the guild had gained with its last two generations of thinkers.

"Look upon this place very carefully, Foit. Emotions

might overwhelm you at these sights—the sound of the water, the splendor of the trees, or the grandeur you might imagine our new hall will achieve once complete. But rather than allow those emotions to flap you like laundry in the wind, you must make yourself like the sail upon a ship instead. Let the emotions pass over you and around you, and most importantly, craft from them only effects of practical import. We cannot cease to feel, but we can be the master of our feelings, rather than their servant."

"Yes, master."

"Come here." Dox walked to the frame of the building and began a lesson in basic geometry. That was more Gomm's area of expertise, but Dox figured and impromptu lesson with a single student would be unlikely to cause an incident. Besides, Mentor Gomm was such a calm, bemused old man.

Foit followed Dox into the structure's interior where Dox drew his student's attention to various angles and planes, also the changing location of the shadows as the sun passed down toward the tips of the western trees.

"Dox!" A voice shouted from the road. A figure approached, his head peaking up over the dip in the road. Student and mentor shared a worried glance, then hurried out of the unfinished Guild Hall toward the approaching man.

The man shouted Dox's name again, panting and stumbling over himself as he approached. Dox recognized him, but had to dig around in his memory to fetch the man's name, eventually arriving at it—Oion. Dox had met him a few times at inter-guild conferences. Oion was a leading figure in the Explorer's Guild, and had many years ago given a fascinating speech comparing the cultures of all the cities of Palípoli, each of which he'd visited and studied in his youth.

"Oion!" Dox approached, placing his forearms together in front of his chest. Foit performed the same gesture of his respect.

Oion attempted the gesture himself, but struggled to hold himself upright, gasping for breath all the while.

"Oion, what is the matter?" Dox said.

"You must— come back— to the city."

Dox looked at Foit askance, and Foit shrugged, equally perplexed. "Has an army arrived? Is the council fighting with itself? Has the city caught ablaze?"

"No," Oion said. "Something... worse."

Foit gulped audibly.

"What could be so horrible?"

"Dervnéss is back," Oion said.

Foit blinked a few time. Dox raced through his memory, at first finding no reference for the name. Eventually, however, he stumbled upon one fragment that seemed to match it. "You don't mean...? Is Dervnéss the man who left Akhtm decades ago to study the peoples in the unknown lands of the faraway north?"

"Yes."

"Gods. He must be... fifty, fifty-five years old or more. You're telling me he has both survived and returned? How is this a catastrophe?"

Oion took a deep breath and finally righted himself. "Because. He has brought new knowledge from those lands."

Dox recognized the confusion roiling within him, and found that even he, for all his training, was struggling to master it.

"Come back to the city," Oion said. "You must hear Dervnéss's story. Perhaps you can save us from what he proposes."

And so Dox allowed Oion, a master of another guild, to lead him back down the hill toward the City of Akhtm, his perplexity growing with every step.

The City of Akhtm lay nestled against the ridges of great mountains which rose up into the north and carried on for many, many thousands of mettrs. They carried on so far, in fact, that no men had settled any lands north of the city. The coast to the south of the city was fertile and the climate very temperate, and so many villages and hamlets dotted it, fueling their powerful protectorate with foodstuffs and livestock both.

With mountains to the north and a natural harbor to its east, Akhtm found itself with few competitors. Sure, rich Meigá lay to the south and militaristic Kholumv east, but great expanses of water separated them from their nearest neighbors, and yet more mountainous terrain divided their lands from those governed by Apmonómen.

Dox was eminently proud of his city every time he looked upon it from the slope of the mountains. Towering constructions of marble sat atop the city's numerous hills, with wooden houses and shops built in the lower lands. From his vantage point upon the descending mountainside, he could even see the metal lanterns which would be lit after sunset and would burn until midnight. Thanks to the many varieties of flower that grew in the nearby mountains and Akhtm's League of Petalharvesters, the fuel for those lanterns would be treated with dyes that allowed their flames to burn with the color of the night's moons. Tonight, being Katkási, they would burn a bright red, the color of the blood blossom, a good match for Atax's violent glow.

But it was daylight still, the sun hanging high above the distant peaks of the western mountains.

Oion led him down into the city in silence, and Foit followed quietly alongside, making eye contact neither with his teacher nor the other guildsman.

They nodded to the watchmen, who waved them in as they passed through the gateway in the stone walls surrounding the city. The street grew immediately boisterous and busy, full of merchants and passing citizens. The sounds of trade and gossip flitted past his ears. Dox scanned the city, searching for telltale signs of worry upon faces, for some cue of shared emotional distress, but his fellow citizens appeared merely to be going about their daily business.

They passed through street after street, the roads growing narrower and narrower, sloping downhill toward the dock. Still, Oion led him forward and Foit followed in his wake.

Dox realized with a start that he had no indication of what this supposed danger was that Dervnéss had brought home with him. His young pupil, he thought, should not be involved until the danger could be assessed.

"Foit," Dox said. "Perhaps you should go home."

"I—"

"Please do as I ask."

Foit nodded, a bit of dejection creeping into his frown and his eyes as he slunk away from them.

"That was for the better," Oion said, once Foit had fallen out of earshot. "I did not want to order away one of your students, but I'm glad you did."

Dox stopped and grabbed Oion by the shoulder. "Tell me what is going on. Or I go no further."

Oion sighed. "Dervnéss has discovered something. New learnings from far away. If we are to believe him—"

"You need not believe." Dox straightened his back. "Surely, we, the learned men of the most learned city in Palípoli can determine truth or falsehood of any matter, no matter its source. I see now why you sought me out." Dox released his shoulder.

Oion looked at him with an expression Dox found hard to read. It was not incredulity exactly, also not quite bemused. Fear definitely played a strong role. The Explorers' Guildsman led him downward still, down a street lined with metal pillar lampposts and then back up the small hill near the port, where the modest but elegant Explorers' Guild lay.

While the rest of the city until now had seemed quite normal, it did not take long for Dox to realize that some disturbance had afflicted the Explorers' Guild. Men ran in and out of the building frantically, and spoke so fast that Dox could not make out more than fractured bits of conversation.

He and Oion walked inside, beneath the structure's marble roof, and the din grew to a roar. A huge group of men stood in a circle at the center of the main chamber, all shouting at once.

"I've brought him!" Oion shouted many times. He pushed through the crowd, guildsmen quieting as they passed, and Dox struggled through their ranks to keep up. Dox's robes of white, which signified the Guild of Reason, stood out quite prominently amongst the many robes of conifer green—the color of explorers.

The crowd grew quieter and quieter, though Dox bumped into many arms and sides and shoulders along the way. The people parted all at once, and Dox spotted a man, a very old, very frail man, his hair all gray and stringy, and his skin very brown, wrinkled, and spotted, sitting in the great marble chair at the center of the commotion. He sat slouched, his emaciated chest struggling to rise and fall, but his eyes shone brightly. Despite his withered frame, great intelligence and power emanated from those eyes, and Dox fixed his gaze onto Dervnéss's.

The crowd grew completely silent.

"I've brought him, Dervnéss," Oion said. "Now tell him. Tell him about the trees."

Dox blinked, his fixed gaze broken. He twisted up his features and turned his skeptical, gaping face to Oion. "Trees? All this over a story about trees?"

"Yes." Dervnéss hefted himself up, standing proudly, albeit hunched over himself. "About the trees. The most important story in all Palípoli. We either heed its warning, or we doom ourselves."

Dox turned his vision back to the elderly guildsman. "Tell your story then."

Dervnéss sat, fixing Dox with an icy stare. Then he nodded. "All right. I will."

You may not know this, Dox, though my fellow guildsmen know it well: My first years as a pupil in this guild were not good. I failed to meet the expectations of my mentor during my first expedition away from Akhtm—a trip to Piirka-Í. I did shoddy work because my heart wasn't in the job, and made excuses to my mentor for not getting the job done. Then, on my second expedition, I botched critical docking negotiations on my first entry into Khatap port. My mentor spent our first day filling out paperwork and bribing the authorities on my behalf.

I took no responsibility for this poor behavior at the time. I was young, arrogant, full of myself, and all too ready to blame others for my own failings.

Upon returning from Khatap, I readied myself to be expelled from the Explorers' Guild. I was filled with venom and spite, and thought of perhaps building a cottage for myself upon the mountainside, isolated from my community, whose bureaucracy I found tedious and unfairly restrictive.

However, I could not rid myself of the guild so easily. My mentor was due one more expedition from me before I could request expulsion. I suspect he wanted to cast me off as much as I wanted to leave, but he must have needed me to perform my duties out of one obligation or another.

I don't know what his reason was, but to this day, I thank the gods that he sent me on that 'final' voyage. He gave me the most monotonous, tedious mission he could think of—that of mapping the coast of the empty wastes south of Zotik-Stheno.

The voyage from Akhtm was long, and all the way through the ports of Meigá and Fid and Épanngel I stewed in my cabin and wrote long, insipid diatribes about the supposed failings of others and how grandeur such as mine was unrecognized in its time.

I burned all those scrolls years ago, lest you think

you might search my belongings for some collateral against my character. I admit I was stupid and obnoxious in those days. But I learned my lessons well.

After Épanngel, we sailed due south, past Zoteno Bay, past the great, brown river Synor. All at once, the trees disappeared and the ground grew from black, to brown, to yellow. It grew cracked, then granular. We had reached the wastes.

I knew right away that something had changed within me. Seeing those vast, empty, desolate tracts of nothing—hills that no man could make fertile, and the scorching sun, which glared more harshly than in the desert flats of Piirka-Í—I realized I was witnessing a thing that was vast and ponderous and, in its own way, utterly grand. I found humility in the realization that so much of our world consists of enormous expanses of land that the gods made unfit for humans.

It was a kind of rapture, and the experience made a true student of me.

I mapped, and I drew, and I detailed the world I had found. I took the remaining paper I owned, for I had wasted much of it on diatribes, and with all my might, I struggled to find the words that would communicate the awe and majesty I had found in those vast wastes. I wanted to find the words that would help my fellow man understand what it was that I had found there, my new awareness of my own smallness, and the humility that had eluded me all my life, and which I had struggled to find without knowing what it was I sought, knowing only that I needed *something*.

As we sailed back to Akhtm, I spent many hours in dialogue with my mentor, who'd been receptive to my change of attitude. After our return, he helped to keep me in the Explorers' Guild, and eventually, he would send me out, for my next mission, to the deserted island Vrach in the eastern reach. The far eastern portion of the island had never been properly mapped.

Such was his trust in my change of heart that he sent me out alone.

Words cannot describe the depth my serenity gained upon this new mission. I sat one glorious night alone under Isórrop's glow, his white light reflecting off pure white sand while desert birds chirped a chorus above my head.

I completed my map of Vrach after only six months, and in exploring the rest of the island, found details of the coast that previous cartographers had missed or erred upon.

I returned, handed in my maps, and won the accolades of my guild. The head master at the time invited me to his home for dinner. He told me that my reputation within the Explorers' Guild had grown to unbelievable heights: 'the young prodigy cartographer of wastelands,' everyone was saying.

He offered me land, money, anything I wanted to secure me for the Akhtm Explorers' Guild and not have me wandering off for another.

I told him that he need not give me land or money to secure my loyalty, only another expanse of desert to explore.

And so I was granted the grandest such task my guild could devise: I was to chart the wastes of the north. All of them, as far as they went. We knew, even then, that some hundreds of mettrs north of Akhtm, the mountains would finally give way to waste, but we knew little else.

I prepared a boat and supplies, stocking up for many months, and then I left.

Did you know, Dox, that before today, the Explorers' Guild has considered me to be 'lost in the pursuit of knowledge' for nearly twenty-four years? Well, here I am! I have survived the northern wastes. Can you all hear me? I have survived!

Beyond the mountainous lands indeed lies waste, but those first cartographers we sent must not have gone very far from where the mountains fell away to sand, for I would find my first great surprise just a day after that transition. The coast veered, turning east into the rising sun. And it was there I found a scene that chilled me, deep into my gut, despite the oppressive heat.

I found stones, arranged upon the ground, a vast network of them, too precisely carved and arranged to have been set there by the gods. No, these desiccated roads were the work of men. They lined a vast area, hundreds upon hundreds of mettrs, going on and on into the horizon, north into the vast sea of sand.

Those roads were old, vastly and ponderously old. Their component stones were worn, and sand had overrun many, but they were certainly roads.

And there was more. Worn pillars of stone stood upon foundations, each pillar's top sanded off to one degree or another. Not a single roof had survived. And the design of the columns resembled neither Akhtm's nor Kholumv's nor that of any other people of Palípoli. These were the architectural skeletons of an ancient and dead people.

I wrote that night—I remember it clearly—under Stathro's turbulent glow, my suspicion that these amazing people had found some way to swell their numbers, to grow powerful and wealthy without the obvious benefit of easy access to food and water. It seemed unreal. How had they accomplished such a thing? A vast network of transportation, perhaps? Had they whole cities of slaves in other, more fertile lands? But then, why colonize the desert? What advantage had it lent them?

At the edge of the ruins, I found a deep, sinuous depression in the sand that ran from the beach northward into the desert. I mapped it, of course, but thought nothing more of it at the time.

I headed back to the edge of the mountains, where the land was rocky and dry, but arable. I found a small wood just a few hundred mettrs inland from the shore and set up camp. This would become my settlement for over five years. I stocked up food during summer and autumn, waited out the winter, which seemed somewhat milder anyway, and then took off into the wastes during the spring.

During my second year I found the remains of two more cities. The first was on the coast further east, and the other lay upon an island south of it. Each of these new ruins consisted of the same strange architecture as the first I had found. I mapped everything, and throughout the entire region, even the island, the sand and blistering heat subsumed everything. I continued to ponder how the people who had once lived here had sustained the number of souls that their remains suggested.

After five years, I had gone out from my camp as far as the duration of the season would allow, perhaps about fifteen thousand mettrs or so. I had charted a total of six ruined cities and had ventured into the desert three or four hundred mettrs across large portions of the mainland. I had fully explored and mapped the two large islands, each with their own city ruins, and had discovered many new desert plants and animals. So much can thrive, even in the desert. But I had yet to meet a single person.

That was about to change.

On the sixth year, I ventured out east past the wastes. I knew I was pushing my luck, but I had decided to see if I could find the end of it all. Sure enough, I passed a small mountain range and a pair of river deltas, and the soil grew blacker and thicker. Trees appeared.

I mapped what I could and headed back to my camp.

I spent that winter eating as little as possible, building myself bows and arrows, and learning to hunt game as best I could. Animals were sparse, but I dried enough rabbit meat to allow me to pack my small ship with a large surplus of food.

I spent my seventh spring sailing as quickly as I could to the new arable land far to the east. Upon arriving, I set up a new camp.

I was not halfway through the winter there, when I woke up one evening to a dreadful start—a wrapping at the door of my hut. I took my knife in my hand, for what little good it would do me, and threw open the door.

A man stood before me, his skin black as pitch, but his eyes wide and scared, much as mine were, I'm sure. Those first few moments were very tense indeed. He held a spear and wore the strangest of attire—we would call his tight-fitting garb women's wear, but among his people this fashion was normal for men.

He took me back to his town and, though I didn't know it at the time, he introduced me to his family and to his village elders. I understood nothing of what was happening and feared throughout the entire affair that I might be maimed or killed at any moment.

But when it became clear that my life was not in danger among them, I persevered and took it upon myself to learn their language. Eventually I came to know his name: Sehhael.

His family invited me into their home and I accepted graciously, preferring his larger space to my hovel in the woods. His home was, as were all other structures in the village, made of stone.

By the end of the winter, I had learned enough of his language to ask about this properly.

"Why do you not make homes out of wood?" I asked. "It would be faster than building everything with stone."

"We fear the wrath of Dzharh Kharza," Sehhael replied.

"Who is Dzharh Kharza?"

He traced his fingers down his arms and then from his chest down his sides. "All in here. The liquid in me is Dzharh Kharza's. The liquid of the trees and the flowers is Dzharh Kharza's."

Many things about their culture became clear to me at that moment—the way they minimally heated their homes, burning the smallest fires possible, and the way they preferred eating plants raw to baking breads and cooking meat. In fact, numerous animals which we eat regularly in Palípoli, such as pigs, lambs, and cows, are called 'bhehes' in Sehhael's land, a word which means something like, 'holy creature.'

During the eighth spring, I did not venture out into the wastes, for I wished to repay Sehhael for the kindness he and his family had shown me. I did, however, describe my adventures and my duty to my homeland to Sehhael. He seemed curious about my explorations, but also somewhat nervous when we spoke of them.

I asked him if his people knew of the people who had lived in the ruined desert cities, and if he knew how so many people had lived in such hot and arid lands without easy access to food and water.

He would say only that the people who had once lived there had not known Dzharh Kharza, and thus did not understand what was happening to them when they tainted their own blood and the blood of the land. I did not understand 'blood of the land,' but it was clear to me that the conversation should go no further. I did not want to upset such a gracious host.

After another productive year of helping Sehhael's family and receiving lodging in return, I reached the ninth spring. I promptly fixed up my little ship and sailed away to the west.

I had grown ever more fascinated with the ruined cities of the waste, and wished to discover what secrets they held. I took up my pencils and turned to sketching everything in sight. When I returned to the village after the voyage of my ninth spring, I worried that my renderings might upset Sehhael, but instead he took a keen interest in them.

"That would have been the governor's mansion," he said. "And that was probably the market square."

"How do you know this?" I asked.

"My people are descended from the people who built these cities," Sehhael said with a tone of melancholy. "The basic patterns have not changed much. But these drawings... I know your heart well, Dervnéss. You are a friend, and I trust you to bring us honor rather than shame, but please do not show these pictures outside our household. Some might misunderstand your fascination with the Dzharh-blasted places."

"Is it... shameful for your people?" I dared.

He responded only with a curt nod. I was even more careful of how and to whom I broached the subject of my discoveries after that.

We proceeded in that manner for three more years. I would go off into the Dzharh-blasted lands during the spring, and in the other months, I lived and worked with Sehhael's family. Every year I brought back more drawings, and every summer Sehhael and I would sit under a large tree they called a shekharch at the edge of his fields and look them over.

"Ah!" he said one day, while looking at two drawings I had done, one of 'Ruined City #2' and another 'Ruined City #4.' "See these pillar stumps here, each arranged in a circle? These were both libraries once. We use the circle to represent knowledge and wisdom. We build the stone circle above the entryway now, but the Dzharh-blasted people put it on the ground, like this."

"I wondered why that building was so large," I said. "It must have housed many scrolls."

"Some think that they did not write on scrolls."

That intrigued me immensely and I encouraged Se-hhael to tell me what he knew.

"I have heard that they wrote on clay," he said. "Such are the stories, anyway. It might be a myth. But a man came through here one year with a huge clay tablet, and it had all these holes poked in it. He said it was an ancient text from the Dzharh-blasted lands about the gods. Some laughed at him and asked him if they could buy it, wanting a thing to hold their children's paint-brushes in."

I knew immediately that I had to scour the ruined libraries for such a tablet.

On the thirteenth spring since I left Akhtm, I ventured out as soon as it was warm enough, and headed directly for 'Ruined City #4,' which lay on an island off the coast. I found the building with the circle of pillars right away, and began hauling off the sand as fast as I could. After a week, I had grown exhausted; my skin was red all over and flaking off my arms, neck, chest, and back. I'd also gone through half my supply of water and nearly exhausted my food.

But I persisted, and three days into my second week, I finally pulled up two half-shards of an enormous clay tablet.

I hefted them back to my ship one at a time under the scorching sun, and expended all my remaining energy sailing myself back to my new home.

Sehhael and I spent the summer and autumn months going over the tablets' markings. With his help, we were able to decipher which indentations in the clay corresponded to which of the sounds of his language. Though their tongue had changed much since those ancient peoples, enough similarity remained that, together, we were able to decipher the meaning of the tablet: it was a list of goods to be traded and their prices.

Over the next seven years, I scoured the ruins and uncovered many more tablets. Sehhael and I would spend our summers translating, and with each clay document we revealed more of the ancient language. During those final years, I began to hear rumors within the village. Word of my adventures in the Dzharh-blasted lands had gotten around, and Sehhael's reputation in the village had fallen as a result. I tried to discuss this with him, suggesting it might be better if I returned to my hut in the woods.

"You are family," he said. "You are the wisest and kindest man I know. You seek knowledge so assiduously. You shall not be alone in your endeavors."

And that was that.

It was on the twenty-first year, as I worried that my body and my reputation in Sehhael's township might both be growing too "blasted" to pursue the endeavor further, that I discovered the final tablet in my growing collection.

It was a complex document—a work order for the

construction of a new zone of houses surrounding a civic hub of some kind. Most interestingly, it ordered the removal of two thousands trees and a clearing of the land. The endeavor was supposed to take ten years—chopping, clearing, construction and all. Using the coordinates given in the document, we were able to place the location of the construction—it was within the 'city limits' of Ruined City #1.

"Are you sure this word means 'tree?'" I pointed and asked. "Could it be 'cactus,' perhaps?" It was a silly question. That waste was so barren that there were not even cacti.

"I can't be sure," Sehhael said. "But I would expect our word for cactus to be theirs as well. This is almost certainly 'tree.'"

"But—" The realization hit me like a marble ceiling caving in overtop my head. The Dzharh-blasted lands possessed no forests now, but they once had. Those lands had become Dzharh-blasted because the people who had lived there had chopped down all of their trees. And most astonishingly, the land and the *weather* had been fundamentally altered as a result.

It may be that the gods declare some places unfit for human life, as with the wastes south of Zotik-Stheno, since, to our knowledge, no humans have ever lived there. However, it is also possible, as with these northern wastes, that human activity, the chopping down of trees, can blight a fertile and prosperous land.

I made plans at once to leave Sehhael's village and return to my true home. I explained to him how my people have no conception of being Dzharh-blasted, in the same way that those ancient people did. Sehhael was upset to see me go, but I also sensed from him, and to a greater extent his wife and sister, the sense of relief that their community lives might return to normal. My adventures were no longer a secret, and being free of the stigma I carried must have been a relief.

And so, on the twenty-second spring I sailed to my first hut at the edge of the mountains, which took some fixing, but functioned adequately enough to keep me warm and fit through the winter, until the twenty-third spring could arrive.

And now, fellow citizens of Akhtm, I find myself here, telling you what I have learned.

Think of what these discoveries imply!

In Palípoli, we know of the ancient gods, our moons—Isórrop, Atax, and Stathro. Atax and Stathro made our world of water and land, and Isórrop made us. So say the ancient legends. Our modern gods are of trees and stones and rivers and clouds, even architecture, commerce, and wisdom. But we have no gods of blood and sap.

This is the wisdom our faraway neighbors to the north have learned: the two substances are the same. Every tree we chop down *taints us*. It is a scar upon the world. We can certainly build many houses without feeling the effects to any noticeable degree. If we leave the mountainside and tracts of wilderness intact, we can be fine for many, many generations.

But how many generations of Palípolians do we intend there to be?

If we chop down *all* the forests, as eventually the people of the Dzharh-blasted lands did many hundreds of years ago, then we can expect the same plague of aridity to infect our beautiful islands. If we do not reign in our desire for more and more wood, our lands will first become dry, then arid, and then ultimately dead.

We will have tainted our own blood. *We* will become Dzharh-blasted ourselves. Or rather, our great-great-great-great grandchildren will.

Dox's hands and fingers surged with tension, and he jammed them behind his back. He stood and gazed cruelly at Dervnéss, who returned his stare with the same simple, stolid sincerity with which he had delivered his monologue.

"Your thesis then," Dox said, expending ever so much effort to keep his voice calm, "is that if we cut down trees, the whole of Palípoli will turn into a desert waste, such as you have seen in the north?"

Dervnéss did not hesitate, nor even so much as quiver. "It is."

"This is a logical fallacy," Dox declared. "We have much evidence to the contrary. All the peoples of Palípoli chop down trees and utilize the wood for warmth and for construction. We have never seen the slightest evidence that the destruction of a tree results in any change in the surrounding land or the local weather."

"The people of Dharaaghe experienced it. They destroyed all their trees, and it destroyed them."

"And Dárag is this desert land of ruined cities?" Dox could feel himself butchering the sounds of the strange language Dervnéss had brought home with him, but decided to try to work his mouth around the strange syllables as best he could without drawing attention to the fact.

"It is its old name, yes," Dervnéss replied. "Sehhael's people call it only the Dzharh-blasted land now."

"Tell me, why did this Seál of whom you speak not return with you to Akhtm?"

"He has a wife, children, a community. Exploring is in my nature, not his."

"And what of these clay tablets you describe?"

"One clay tablet is as big as this." Dervnéss held out the thumb and forefinger of each of his hands, forming a rectangle half a mettr long, and the height of Dervnéss's entire torso. "And as thick as my fist, too. I left the tablets with Sehhael as food and water made for more practical companions on my trip home."

"How convenient for you."

"My story is true."

Dox sighed, and immediately thought he would have

done better to hide his exasperation. That had been a tactical and a logical error. He strove again to set his emotions aside.

"Dervnéss," Dox said. "It is clear you mean well for us. Your maps and charts and descriptions of these people far to the north will certainly make excellent additions to our libraries. You have helped secure Akhtm's role as the most literate and knowledgeable city in Palípoli, despite what others might say of us. That said, I humbly suggest that your... fondness for Seál and his people may have clouded your logic on this matter. These ancient superstitions you speak of—'Dár-blasted' and gods of sap—these are not the basis for logic and reason. These are not even the true gods of our lands. Perhaps these other lands had other gods who were offended in some way—"

Dervnéss stood up and glared down at Dox. "Are the gods perfection incarnate?"

"Of course."

"Is our entire world made from them?"

"Yes."

"Then how could it be that some lands have some gods, while some lands have others?"

Dox's ember of rage seared hot red, and before he could tamp it down, he allowed himself to shout back at his opponent. "You dare to speak of gods! You admit to having worshipped those of a foreign land for over a decade, and then you dare to come back here and insult both logic and our city's very economic foundation by suggesting that the felling of a tree can turn soil to sand! This is the most idiotic conversation I have ever had!"

The moment the words were out of his mouth, he knew he had erred. The term 'ad hominem' jumped to the forefront of his mind—an argument based on an attack of character rather than utilization of logic and reason.

"Ad hominem," a voice said. The gathered crowd turned, to where a young man stood at its periphery. Foit had spoken the words. His eyes glistened with tears. "Ad hominem, master. You taught me that term."

Dox stared, spellbound. He had no response for his pupil. He felt shame, an emotion he had not felt for a very, very long time.

"Even if your case is logical, it's not practical," An Explorers' Guildsman shouted up to Dervnéss. "Do you expect us to let our homes stay cold in the winter, and to stockpile berries instead of meat and bread?"

"I'm not going to do that," shouted another guildsman. "I've got a family to feed!"

"My son is an infant," shouted yet another. "He'll die if I don't keep him warm!"

The grand chamber erupted into the same uproarious, overlapping conversation Dox had witnessed upon entering. He realized, only then, that he could not roll back his fallacy. The conversation that had existed on his terms, terms of logic and reasoning, had ended, and he had been the one to end it.

He backed out of the chamber, pushing through Explorers' Guildsmen and growing ever more frantic as he struggled to be free of the shouting crowd.

Dox dared to take one last look out at the men standing around a beaming Dervnéss, who sat triumphantly atop his marble throne. The old man smiled snidely back. As Dox turned back toward the exit and the flickering red illumination of evening, his eyes glimpsed past Foit's face.

The look of disappointment was unmistakable.

Dox exited the city and climbed the mountain, back upward to Ígia. He carried with him a torch he had taken from the guards as he had exited the city. It was not entirely safe to venture outside the walls so late, but thoughts of safety were far from his mind just then.

He climbed and climbed. The sunlight waned, disappearing behind the distant western mountains. A flat expanse of farmland in the valley glowed momentarily golden under the setting sun until it turned crimson, then indigo. Dox climbed through the dark, the torch his sole illumination. Its light danced amongst the trees, and nighttime insects began to chirp as he passed.

The details of his journey seemed starker somehow. It was as though his fit of emotion before Dervnéss in the Explorers' Guild had loosed a deluge of others. Every detail of the mountainside had grown vivid. His soul ached with every flicker of light and shadow, with every buzz, chirp and squawk.

The road flattened out, and he drew near Ígia. He looked upon the skeleton of the new guild hall. Just hours ago, it had seemed a grand monument to reason. He saw now only hollow supports—logs suspending some edifice of human construction that held no more meaning for him.

'And it's all made of wood, too,' he thought.

"Dox?"

Dox turned and held the torch aloft.

A familiar, old, and friendly face shone forth, another torch suspended above it as well.

"Gomm!" Dox called out. He walked toward his colleague. "You shouldn't be out here at night all alone."

Gomm chortled. "You were never good at heading your own advice."

"I guess not. You heard about Dervnéss, then?"

Gomm nodded, then laughed louder. "You botched that one good."

Dox turned and walked back toward the skeleton of the guild hall.

"Hey!" Gomm called to his back. "I'm not going to lie and tell you everything will be all right, but in the grand scheme of things, this is hardly the worst thing a guild member has done. Remember when Iotelo told the entire council to go to Ahdez?"

Dox couldn't help but laugh at that. Gomm joined

him as he strode toward the new hall.

"One of my students was there."

Gomm furrowed his brow. "Why on earth did you allow that?"

"I didn't. He snuck in and hid amongst the crowd."

Gomm shook his head. His silver beard swayed comically under the torchlight. "Damn kids. You included." Gomm punched Dox in the arm.

"I've always wondered, are you this much of a... goofball with your students?"

"Depends on the group I'm teaching."

"I figured as much. What do you think of Dervnéss's story?"

Gomm released a long sigh and scanned his eyes over the skeleton of the guild hall. "I think that I don't have enough information to say one way or the other."

"Trees changing the land and the weather if they're chopped down? It just seems so ludicrous—"

Gomm grabbed Dox's shoulder and turned him. "And if you could go back in time and tell your great-great-great-great grandfather that you were going to have a three story guild hall built out of lumber upon a mountainside?"

"I suppose, but—"

"Is it possible that trees breathe with their leaves, the same way we breathe through our mouths?"

Dox blinked a few times. "Perhaps."

"And is possible that the trees roots affect the soil

they ensnare?"

"… Yes."

"I can declare certainty about none of these things." Gomm turned back to the guild hall. "No man can. In light of that, I am merely open to the possibility that the things Dervnéss says could be true."

"Open enough to cease construction here at Ígia?"

Gomm smirked into the night. "No. But I believe, that *that*, young man, is the worry that incensed you enough to override your composure today."

"I'm not young anymore. I shouldn't make such stupid mistakes."

"Perfection is for the gods. Speaking of which, how about a drink? Let's get out of here before we're mugged."

Dox took a deep breath and nodded. "Okay."

"Don't worry about Ígia," Gomm said as they descended down the mountain path. "Solutions abound. Our concession to Dervnéss, should he find any support on the council, (which I suspect will be difficult for him at best) will be as such: we will maintain an orchard on the property, granting both trees to the land and a diet filled with raw fruit to us humans. In addition, we will keep one instruction room unheated year-round."

Dox let out a laugh. "Mine, I suppose."

"Absolutely." Gomm slapped him on the back.

"I admit," Dox continued chuckling. "I deserve that."

"What is that metaphor you're so fond of?" He

dropped the pitch of his voice to a deeper baritone than usual. "The laundry and the sail, right?"

"Yeah."

"Remember that even a sail cannot be turned directly into the wind. You should use that in your lessons."

Dox was very glad it had been Gomm to come fetch him.

"I suppose," Dox said, "that seems logical enough. For tonight, at least."

Gomm's broad smile glowed in the torchlight. "My boy, don't tell the pupils, but that's all the logic we've ever really needed."

THE MEASURE

I still do not know if this tale bears repeating, and I must admit a significant hesitation, that at some time in the future, some details within these pages may serve to identify and thus indict one of my colleagues or their descendants, and thus bring ruin upon them. I have taken care to eliminate as many such details as I can, but just as it seems that one speck of dust sometimes remains after a thorough washing, I fear that some lingering, seemingly benign word or phrase may serve as a link to my associates.

For my part, whether or not I am discovered is of no great importance. The citizens of Sóf know my positions quite well.

Our inquiry, for whatever it is worth to future generations, has never been malign. We merely wish to better reveal the truth of the world to human minds, and help us all live better, happier, more righteous lives. If this goal is impious, then I willingly accept the brand of "heretic," knowing it means not what those who sling it suppose it to.

Despite the risk, I have decided that this story should be told.

As my public body of works shall attest, I have spent a good deal of my life in quiet study. Although I have on occasion taken part in debate with Krateé or Risto at the Scholastic Plaza, I suspect these dialogues will go unremarked, for, while others, especially Krateé, revel for hours in endless lines of verbal questioning with others, my goal has been the transcription and transmission of my thoughts. If you are reading this, then it means that I am no more, and you will have full access to the works of my entire lifetime.

I have written this in secret near the end of my life. I do not expect to produce anything further (though I will not state it impossible). Though this is temporally the last of my works, these scrolls you hold in your hands are best read after *On Moral Responsibility* and before *Our Responsibility to Others*. The recurrence of the word "responsibility" in their titles is intentional, and, I believe, if it were not for this present work, it might never have become clear how my mind made the leap from the one to the other.

In *On Moral Responsibility*, I made the claim that man is the measure of all things. By this, I meant that human reason was the very basis of moral judgment. Morality, I argued, was fluid. Since perception dictated the form of morality, and since individuals' perceptions differed, morality, via transitive association, could be based on individual views and individual situations.

This stance led me into a dangerous and inescapable conundrum. By making man the measure of all things, it next struck me that perhaps this position could undermine the very gods themselves. I was shaken very deeply by this possibility. There was a two-year interval between my two treatises on responsibility, and during that interval, I very carefully sought the answer to a very dangerous question: If human perception dictates morality, and if human reason is the sole basis of the world as it is, then does this not do away with the gods? Under this new view, "god" is reduced to a supremely functional human intellect. Rather than coming down from heaven and blessing the just and punishing the wicked, "man is the measure of all things" extends the word "all" to encompass heaven and hell. When I first arrived at this idea, I did not quite intend it to go so far, and I was horrified at this conclusion when it occurred to me.

I decided I needed help to untangle the moral and ethical mess I had made. I gathered up associates I could trust, and we met at my house once a week for over a year. It was the only time in my life when my writing ceased and dialogue flowed furiously between me and other Sófan thinkers. I remember it being an anxious time for me. I worried constantly that important thoughts and ideas might be slipping away from me, but I dared not capture them on the page, and thus accidentally record impiety.

We had begun early in the winter, and I remember, when it began to grow cold at the end of that first year, I wondered if perhaps I should simply "roll back" my philosophy to before *On Moral Responsibility*. I considered burning that document and beginning afresh. I made a few fits and starts of replacing that treatise on paper, but I could not escape my proposition that man is the measure of all things. I would attempt to write around it, and then suddenly find myself staring at that same conclusion again.

Unsure of what to do next, I asked my friends for help at one meeting in the dead of that second winter.

A and T shrugged. M frowned and looked at the wall.

"M," I said, "If there's something that you know could help, please say it. I beg you. I cannot proceed with my work until this issue is resolved."

He let out a sigh, then looked at me with furtive

eyes. "There's a librarian friend of mine. Actually, he's a friend of my son-in-law. They came over for a dinner party we threw the other night. Someone asked him about the Dark Archive. The usual question, you know, 'why do we keep around books we know to contain evil words?' And, I remember remarking this, because normally librarians respond with the usual, 'we must keep evil in sight, though at a distance, so we can recognize it when it encroaches upon us anew.' Instead, he said something like, 'Which is the greater evil, to destroy evil words, or to use them against themselves, so that they might come to serve another master? There are even books that may blur and bend the very definition of the words 'good' and 'evil,' and though the world is not yet ready for such upheaval, it may one day require those insights in order to survive. The Dark Archive does not only keep wicked things from seeing the light of day, it prevents the current wickedness in the world from prematurely destroying the seeds of future greatness.'"

A and T were now looking at M quite intensely, as was I. My mind roiled. Such a man as this might be trusted with our secret. It was a huge risk, and that was the focus of all my thoughts. I don't think I ever considered, in that moment, that this librarian might actually divulge some occult book to me that would mend my predicament.

A shook his head. "It's way too dangerous. How can we be sure—?"

"He works with my son-in-law," M said. "I can make sure.[†]"

And so, one week later, the Librarian showed up at my door. We would meet just before dusk, and I know it must have been the 14th or 15th when he appeared, because, to this day, I retain a vivid memory of the deep red sky of dusk thanks to a full Atax, basking my doorsteps in crimson light, and this young man, probably not much older than twenty-two or twenty-three, pulled down his hood and shook a long, scraggly mop of hair. His countenance seemed to drop upon seeing me; to this day I do not know in what way I failed to meet his expectations. We did not talk much after the events I am to relate here.

He came in, and we began. I ran him through the basics of the philosophy of "man is the measure of all things," and how this leads to the querulous situation of human intellect replacing our deities in heaven. I summarized my failed attempts to back up and reverse the position, but as it stood, I needed either to refute my own argument or find some other logical escape from my intellectual quagmire.

I remember, he nodded toward M, then looked directly at me with a hesitant, almost mournful gaze. When he spoke, it was as though he struggled to force the

[†]If you go searching for an associate of mine who had a librarian son-in-law, you will find no one. I have intentionally changed the relationship between M and the Librarian.

words from his lips. "M described your predicament to me, and I believe I have a solution of sorts."

I struck my forearms together, bowed to him, then clasped his hands in mind. "My young friend, if you have the knowledge of a remedy, please share it. I don't care where it comes from—"

At that, he jerked his hands out of mine. "Stand up," he spoke harshly, and I did so. "Do not thank me for this. For anyone but M here, I would not be doing this now. You have no idea what you are asking of me—what you are actually wishing to know."

"Is this knowledge really so terrible?" I asked.

He cast me a look at me as a parent might to a child's particularly ignorant question. "Perhaps. I will let you judge for yourself." He reached into the satchel slung over his shoulder and retrieved a worn, leather-encased tome. It was average in size. A leather band fastened it together. He handed it to me, and I took it, turning it over.

"Is this from the Dark Archive?" I asked.

"It is."

"Where did it come from?" I pulled at the leather strap until it gave way from its loop.

"Kholumv," the Librarian said.

I pulled open the covers, and number of brownish pages appeared, their edges wrinkled with water-dam-age. Across the front page and the edges of the pages lay a smear of blood, dried black with age.

"It was found on Kholumv Isle's northwest shore," the Librarian continued. "It was wrapped and sealed on a rock, some ways away from the water, but rain must have still seeped in. We don't know how long it sat there before it was found."

I flipped past the first blood-spattered page and scanned over the second. "A journal?"

The Librarian nodded.

"May I read aloud?"

Another nod, this one more apprehensive.

I turned around, checking that the front door and the door to the slaves' quarters were sealed. Then I cleared my throat and began.

The first section of entries seemed unremarkable to me. They were written in pencil. The hand was elegant, even a bit stylish, perhaps a bit too exaggerated for my taste. But I remember it struck me as lacking pomposity.

DÉKKAD 13

We arrived in Kholumv today. Ekil eyed the working women, as usual, and wondered out loud how long until we could go to the pubs. Tiím told him not until after we'd made contact. We spent the next four hours searching the city, jumping from market to market, looking for the sign. Ekil grew more agitated all the time. He got that way, on ships. Not usually women on board, so when we make port he has to let loose.

It was Tiím who spotted the contact—a shrouded figure in a dark alleyway who made the hand gesture. We split up and converged on the alley one at a time, so as not to draw attention. It was here that we discovered our target and our means of entry. Our contact pointed to a rubbish bin, and we raided it, discovering satchels, one prepared for each of us. Then he handed us each a purse of coins, nodded, and went on his way.

At the hostel, Ekil threw his satchel on the ground and made for the door.

"You at least need to try that on before you go get laid," I said.

Ekil grumbled but complied, yanking the robes out of his sack and throwing them on both inside-out and askew. "There," he said. "Nice and holy-like. Can I go fuck now?"

Tiím tried his on, examined himself, then stripped and climbed into his bed without a word. I stay up by candle writing this.

DÉKKAD 14, MORNING
We woke up refreshed. Ekil was noticeably less agitated. We ate breakfast silently, then, wearing our normal clothes, we went to the market to buy supplies.

I was lucky early. I found a trader selling traveling supplies, and he had nearly everything I needed: a water skin, dried meat, dried berries, extra pencils, and more.

"You heading out of town?" The trader eyed my selections warily.

"Yeah," I said.

"You realize it's the fourteenth, right? Katkási."

"Yes…" I drew the sound out, mildly confused.

"Most locals don't head out on the road on Katkási."

"I'm going with a group. We can handle brigands."

"It's not that. It's just, you know our local deities, right? You've heard of Pollem?"

"Of course. What of it? Does the god himself make war on Katkási?"

"You might say that. He does not take kindly to travelers of his isle under Atax, least of all when Atax stands alone in the sky."

"I will find his shrine then, and say a prayer. That should be enough to appease Pollem, eh?" I threw in a smile for good measure.

The trader did not smile back. "Do as you will. But I, for one, would not trifle with the gods, Pollem least of all."

When I returned to the hotel, the others had not yet arrived. Tiím will be by soon. I expect Ekil to want one more good lay before we head out. We will change into monks' robes before leaving the city. I hope Ekil does not hold us up too long.

DÉKKAD 14, EVENING

Our departure from the city was uneventful. The streets grew vacant as we approached the city limits, and we easily found an alley where we could change into our robes. We proceeded north on the coastal road perhaps fifteen thousands mettrs or so, and made camp by the side of the road as the sun set.

Ekil took off his robes and decided to go off hunting. Once he was out of earshot, Tiím suggested that he was instead trying to find a private place to wank. This prompted a conversation in which I discovered that Tiím doesn't much care for Ekil's promiscuous behavior, in as much as he treats women badly. I had already noticed one incident a while back. We'd been at a pub, and Ekil had taken one of the women upstairs. She emerged some time later, bruised and bawling, followed by a raging Ekil. I had had to pay off the barkeeper, who was none too happy with us. Tiím had not spoken to Ekil for over a day, and had maintained a distance from him for longer.

After a moment of hesitation in our conversation, Tiím mentioned, quite abruptly, that he'd been married once, but his wife had died in childbirth, and the child had been stillborn. "Most men revere the gods and treat their women like they treat their cattle," he'd said. "I revered her."

I tried to think of the right way to show the subject due respect, and thus get more out of him, but at that moment, Ekil returned with three dead squirrels, and we cooked our dinner instead.

DÉKKAD 15

We reached the intersection where the western coastal road meets the road through the northern interior. We began into the interior and walked about an hour or so before sunset.

Ekil hunted for our dinner again.

DÉKKAD 16

Another full day of walking and nothing unusual to report. We're making great time. I expect we are over halfway to the shrine, which is built into the north face of the mountains and overlooks the northern forests. The path has already begun to climb.

Ekil continues to hunt for our food.

I find it a bit odd that we haven't met anyone else at all on the road. Even with the god's proscription against traveling during Katkási, I should expect to see at least some travelers moving about the region. As it is, this is a happy occurrence for us. Each passerby is potentially a witness, and with no passersby, we can focus our attention on other things.

DÉKKAD 17

When I awoke today, I went to relieve myself in the forest, and as my drowsiness wore off, for the first time I noticed something odd about the local flora. The bark, the branches, and the leaves of the trees have been invaded by some kind of blue-green blight. It looks puffy and also bristly. It is like nothing I have ever seen.

I worried that, in my drowsiness, I'd blundered into some blighted part of the forest, and so hurried back to the camp site, but discovered that all of the trees there had been blighted, too. I roused Ekil and Tiím, who also marveled at this development, both saying they had never seen or heard of anything like it before.

We decided to travel onward, as the blight has not affected us. We each checked ourselves over carefully. We also decided not to eat the plants or game of the forest, since we have enough food in reserve to make it back to Kholumv.

It was at lunchtime that I again remarked the trees. The patches of blight were getting larger, and they'd begun growing on the grasses and underbrush as well. We found a dry, rocky area to pitch the tents, but we decided against a fire, as we didn't want to burn any of the blight, and thus turn it into air and inhale it.

Another bad turn awaited us. We found a stream just before dark, and Ekil almost put his skin into it, but I stopped him. The water of the stream had a blue-green tint. To me, this was the most unnatural sight of all. I had heard of diseases that affected trees and plants rather than animals and humans. But this blight was apparently also capable of infesting itself into the very water of the earth. Would it proceed out into the oceans and taint the life source of the world?

We checked our water supply when we got back to

camp. Five full skins remaining amongst the three of us. One of those Ekil had filled yesterday. Tiím wondered at its safety, even if it had filled it before we had seen any of the blight. And, of course, Ekil wasn't sure which one it had been.

I urged us to perhaps abandon our task. Surely our employers would accept the explanation and a minor payment to make good on our promise of a second attempt, or the selection of a new target in another land. Tiím objected. He suggested that our employers would grant us no such understanding and that we were liable to be the object of suspicion of sneaking the gains away for ourselves. Furthermore, we could mix our two skins of wine in with the water, and thus make it safe to drink. I objected that, while that worked with many forms of pollution, there did exist those that resisted wine-purification. I insisted that we dump all the water we had, not knowing which could contain the blight, and refill them only upon exiting the infested part of the forest. In the meantime, the two skins of wine we possessed would have to suffice. Ekil agreed with Tiím that we should proceed with the mission, and with me about dumping our water.

I write these words in the dying light of the sun on one side, and the purplish glow of Atax and Stathro, who appear unusually close together in the sky this evening. I have never been a devout man, not even close, given my occupation, but I can't but wonder at the fact, which I've just realized, that we will be attempting to exit the blighted region of this forest on Kens.

In this journal entry, the hand changes somewhat. It is still clearly the same writer, but he seems to lose control of his pencil at moments, jerking it nervously this way and that. Given what I discovered within, that is understandable.

DÉKKAD 18

I know not if I can   I have been running. I don't know how long. Part of me wants to pick up and run again. Can there be any use in recording these terrible things I have witnessed today? Will I even be able to?

I will try.

The road remained deserted, and it was this morning, I think, that I remarked that I no longer heard birds in the trees. I had been wondering for some time as to what was causing my unease, and all at once I had realized that that familiar background sound was entirely absent.

We also witnessed a large clump of blue-green blight fall from a tree branch to the road some ten mettrs in front of us. It did not splatter or disperse on impact. Rather, it remained a contiguous clump and wobbled a bit, about the size of a human fist. We hurried around it, but I could tell from Tiím's gait that even he was having second thoughts about our decision to proceed onward.

But we did proceed onward, and it was sometime after noon that we came to Pollem's Shrine. Or perhaps it was before noon. As I said, I don't know how long I've been running. Too long. And wine does not parch the thirst of one who has exhausted himself so.

The temple

Words cannot describe but I will try.

The blight had attached itself to the wooden parts of the shrine, and where it touched them, they seemed to sag, even melt. At least half of the surfaces were covered. This part was unsurprising, as we had already witnessed as much with the trees, but truly frightening to discover was that the blight could attach itself to metal as well. The lamp posts lining the entryway to the shrine sagged and hung over the path at a cacophony of angles. One candle had fallen out of one and lay on the path before us.

We walked silently through this and up to the central shine structure. Its supports had partially given way, causing the ceiling to droop in a number of places. The whole front facade seemed to be teetering over us, ready to collapse at any moment. And most horrible, the images of Pollem, three of them, two statues on either side of the entrance, one carved into a stone plate above it, all were covered with blight, which had distorted Pollem's features and caused them to sag, making his face appear that of a demon's.

The entrance stood still, although the frame around it looked precariously weak. It appeared to me an abyss.

I remember, I began to form an argument in my mind, a sentence, how I would convince the others to head back, to give up on this, to not enter this place thoroughly contaminated with evil. But I never spoke those words, for a cry rang out from within the shrine: human, female, pained, somewhat gurgling.

We cast glances between one another and the entrance to the shrine. Not one of us said a word.

Another horrible cry, the same voice, but tainted again with that quite unnatural liquid quality.

"That sounds like…" Tiím said softly. He let the sentence remain unfinished.

"Tiím…?" The voice from within the shrine called out. "Tiím…?" Again.

He lurched forward, and I grabbed his arm. "Do not go in there!" I commanded, quite unsure where I had gotten my resolve, but in that moment, I had it.

He tried to pull himself out of my grasp, and I grabbed harder. "Damn it, that's her. Let go—!"

"Tiím!" The voice. "It hurts it hurts it hurts it hurts—" And this devolved into a horrible, bubbly, sloshing noice, whose pitch descended out of the feminine register and then out of the human register entirely.

"It's her!" Tiím found such strength as to push me to the ground. "She's still alive!"

"No," Ekil said, grabbing Tiím by the arm and fortifying his stance. "This is something else."

Tiím screwed up his face. I, meanwhile, had righted

myself, and had grasped his other arm anew.

"It can't be her," I said. "You told me how she died. You saw her, didn't you? You saw how it happened?"

"Tiím!" Another gurgling wail. "Help me!"

Tiím's eyes burst tears, and he shook his head. He struggled only momentarily against us, but we held him fast.

"We need to turn around," I said, "and leave this place now."

The shrine structure itself punctuated my statement with a groan, some interior part of it having perhaps become unstable. The sound of creaking wood was followed by a sharp splintering, then a small crash, as if something ceramic had fallen to a stone floor and shattered.

"Tiím!" the voice shouted, as urgent as ever.

Tiím sniffled, his voice a whisper. "It sounds like her."

"It's not," Ekil urged.

A deep breath from Tiím. "Can I pick up my pack?"

Ekil and I shared a look.

"You're right," Tiím said. "We need to get as far away from here while there's still light."

We released his arms. I want to believe that he had not deceived us, but the next events happened so fast, that it's hard to tell. He did seem to be starting to turn himself back toward his fallen belongings, but it couldn't have been more than a few moments since we released him that sharp crashes erupted from within the shrine, not sounds of the building collapsing, but something within the building colliding with the structure. Then there were footsteps, and then, from the dark entrance appeared a woman with long, black hair, wide, red eyes, her arms, legs, torso and face, splotched with the blight. She reached an arm out toward us, and then shouted Tiím's name, but her head craned unnaturally backward, and that horrible gurgling sound seemed to ring off the mountainside and pierced my ears. All of her seemed to be pulled back inside the shrine as she did this, and it was then that Tiím took off toward the shrine screaming, his words incomprehensible, if they were words at all, and he disappeared into the black portal which had recently suctioned in the blighted visage of a woman.

"Tiím!" Ekil and I both shouted after him, watching him disappear into that terrible place.

We remained silent for a few moments after he entered. We heard the scuttle of feet against wood. Then a crash. Then another groan from the structure itself. Then a long, long silence.

"Tiím?" I called out.

Many moments of no response.

Ekil grabbed my arm. "We take his stuff and we head back now. Who is this woman to him, anyway?"

I shot him a terrible grimace. "His dead wife."

"Dead? Then this place really is Ahdez erupting forth on earth, and I'm not staying here a—"

A deep, masculine, groaning, gurgling cry of pain

erupted from the shrine complex, followed by steps, but at an awkward, unnatural rhythm. One step, pause, two more, pause, one more, one more, pause, two more…

"Tiím?" I tried to call out again, but my voice caught in my throat and claimed the second syllable entirely.

Another groan, and then a hand appeared, grasping the door frame, right overtop one of the pustules of blight. Tiím's body appeared at the entrance. He was nearly naked. Tatters of his clothes clung to his body. His skin had become translucent, a blue-green translucence. His eyes bulged. He reach out toward us and opened his mouth and groaned, and then… then… how can I even write this? His body… lost cohesion entirely. His jaw fell from its hinge. His outstretched arm drooped, detached, fell and splattered on the ground. He stumbled over the stairs and crashed to dirt, exploding into a pool of goo. His organs, wholly visible, melted into the rest of the blue-green gore that had been him, and only his bones and his skull remained unmelted, suspended in that awful miasma. They stuck up out of that mess of him, his ribcage, and femurs, and—

I think Ekil shrieked.

I know I shrieked.

We ran. We both began running. And we ran until we couldn't run anymore. I don't know if I stopped him, or if he stopped me.

We ran, and then we stopped running. And now, I am writing.

I don't want to write about today anymore.

From this point forward, the writing gets progressively sloppier. Toward the end of the section, his pencil seems to veer off in a straight line toward the edge of the page mid-word for no apparent reason.

ENTÉKKAD I

When I awoke this morning, Ekil was already up. We had not made a fire, since we dared not burn the tainted wood. He sat in the road, facing away from my tent. I called out to him, and he, stood, turning slowly so that I could see that he was still himself. But it only grew more awkward after that. We had a brief conversation about whether or not traveling on Kens or remaining in the vicinity of the shrine would be the greater evil. We decided to keep traveling.

I exhausted my half of the wine today.

Despite the distance we've covered, the blight seems to have only grown stronger. I spotted a whole tree encased in the blue-green, and most trees now are at least half-covered. We habitually dodge clumps of the stuff on the road, fallen from overhanging tree branches.

The streams of the forest remain blue-green, and we dare not drink the water. I wish we still had the wine, for I am now desperate enough that I would mix it with water from the streams if I could.

Ekil and I did not converse during our journey. I

don't think either of us wants to talk about Tiím, though perhaps we should. He was the best of the three of us. I think, from what little I know about his life, that when his wife died, he lost his faith entirely. What horror could it be to rob the temples of the gods, when the gods have already robbed from you any prospect of happiness? I suppose some wise man of Sóf might argue that Tiím needed to realize that other kinds of happiness were still possible. I think they don't realize how ludicrous that sounds to someone who once loved, but for whom that love is now wholly impossible. If there existed gods who cared about mankind, there would not be such horrors in the world, let alone what we witnessed yesterday.

At the very least, Tiím, your suffering is over.

Entékkad 2

We are growing weak from lack of water. My throat has become so terribly parched, and perhaps it is dehydration and lack of sleep—I have not been sleeping well—and perhaps we are not traveling very far, but the forest keeps going, and the blight grows stronger it is now rare to see bark or leaves. I don't know we are moving and going, but so thirsty.

A clump hit me today. It fell from a tree and scream and tore off my clothes right on the left shoulder. I look at my shoulder even now and nothing appears the matter but I abandoned my jacket that I wore and I was cold, but I have my sleeping sack wrapped around me now. We are camped in the middle of the road. Everywhere else is trees, and those are dangerous now. Ekil has not loaned me a jacket we do not talk much.

We should be at the coast by now. Unless we didn't actually run that far? But we ran for so long.

Also, I realized just as I sat down to write, that I have not glimpsed Isórrop through the branches today. Maybe he is near the horizon. But all day?

Entékkad 3

Looked for Isórrop all day. Was more attentive to the sky. Did not see him.

We have been on this path too long. We should be near the coast by now. We must be so close.

I noticed today that clumps of blight are flaking off of the bulbous blue masses of trees and grasses that they now encase completely. The flakes waft through the air around us, an awful blue-green snow that never quite falls to earth.

"We are breathing it," I said to Ekil, when I noticed this. He did not respond we have not spoken since I don't remember. I don't know anymore.

Where is Isórrop? The sun has set and risen twice since Kens and I would not write in my journal if the sun hadn't set and risen how could it still be Kens? Where is Isórrop?

Tomorrow will be Ármon and Stathro at least will show herself and her light will be visible against the trees yes that must be it because Isórrop's light is white it is harder to see and but it was dark last night and there was no light in the sky and there were no clouds when was the last time I saw clou

Across the second page of this next entry, there are circular splotches that warp the paper.

Entékkad 4

I was not able to find Isórrop or Stathro today. It remains Kens even though it has been three days since Kens. Perhaps that is why we walk interminably and do not reach the intersection. This road was not so long on the way here but our environment is so changed that it is hard to compare the land around us to the one we passed through on the way here.

Everything is now completely encased in the blight. Flakes of it waft through the air. It is no longer possible to walk around the clumps on the road. We simply tread over them I am wearing my sleeping bag as a jacket I should not have abandoned my jacket that was stupid.

A long time ago Ekil said that Ahdez had erupted on earth I think he's right I have known for a long time because of my brother. Because it was my fault. The gods know I have never forgiven myself but it's not enough for the gods to know you have to suffer on earth on earth earth oh gods I was just a boy! Can you really hate a boy and make him suffer for so long because of a stupid mistake, a dumb lack of courage in one so young but with such terrible consequences there it was my fault it was my fault that my brother was sold off as a slave and I stayed free because I couldn't stand the idea of slavery and I did it I did it I did it not him there are you happy now can I leave this awful forest now my fault it was my fault my fault let him go let him go please I'll be the slave as long as it takes, just let us leave this horrible place where it's always Kens and everything is alive and not alive and everything is wrong and please just let him go he shouldn't be suffering anymore for my mistakes because it was my fault and not his and I'll never touch your shrines and temples ever again and I'll tell my associates that I'm done even though they'll probably find a way to kill me and please make it stop and set him free set him free just set him free please set him free *(three illegible lines)*

We drank the water.

ENTÉKKAD 5

Today should be Ármon, but still no sign of the moons. We ate through the last of our food. Even if we wanted to eat something from the forest, nothing edible remains. The only natural-appearing things we see anymore are the streams. Everything else is completely encased in blight. The blue branches hang over us with their tufts seem to be telling us we are next.

We should not be far from the coast but I know we'll

just keep walking we know it's pointless but we keep trudging I with my sleeping bag wrapped around me like an idiot I deserve this that's the thing is I know I deserve this.

It's Ármon today, but no moons in the sky.

ENTÉKKAD 6
Glorious moons our gods! began the old prayers that way, the old times before all the new gods when our ancestors worshipped the moons as gods and today Isórrop, Stathro, and Atax should be together in the sky Isórrop Stathro Atax. Atax, man. Stathro, woman. Isórrop, the holy bond that binds them like that was ever important to me, a man who let his poor brother be sold into slavery when he knew damn well that it should have been [illegible] Some things are too terrible for a person to bear alone and a whole life is not thick enough to absorb all that pain so we have to lash out in other ways like stealing from temples tit for tat. Gods, you think can fuck with me? Well I'll pay you one right back. Take that. One should not plays such games with the gods.

ENTÉKKAD 7
This is Ahdez. [illegible]

ENTÉKKAD 8
How many days of Dikhon after Makhí? [illegible] How many days of Dikhon after Makhí? Is it two or three? [il-

legible] I think it's three, but it might be two. HOW CAN IT STILL BE KENS?

ENTÉKKAD 9
[illegible] I think Ekil is going to try to kill me.

ENTÉKKAD 10
[illegible]

The illegible scrawling beneath the final entry is spattered with blood.

I closed the journal, wrapped its leather flaps around the pages, slipped the strap through its loop, and set the thing gently down on the table in front of me. My living room remained silent, and the others stared at me, expectant. I shook my head. "It is an evil book."

The Librarian nodded slowly and bit his lip. "Yes. But what has it taught you?"

I shook my head. "Too much within it doesn't make sense. Are we to believe that the gods destroyed an entire temple, all of its presumably innocent priestesses and suppliants, and its forest for thousands of mettrs around, just to ensure divine retribution against three minor criminals?"

The Librarian chuckled. "If only it were as simple as that. As I said, this journal was discovered on the Northwest shore of Kholumv Isle. We were lucky that it was a

Sófan expedition that found it. Any others probably would have burned it. They immediately sailed on to Kholumv City and informed the authorities of what it described as having happened to Pollem's shrine. The city officials organized the Aquatic Legion into well-equipped expedition parties and sent them forth to all three shrines in the northern reaches of the isle—the shrines to Hom, Púrkai, and Pollem. Each party returned three days later and reported that their target shrines had appeared intact. None reported any sign of blight in the wilderness, and none of the priestesses at any of the shrines reported any disturbances or unusual incidents even remotely matching the descriptions in the journals. Travelers on the roads reported nothing out of the ordinary, either. In short, no one on Kholumv could find any evidence to support the notion that the events of this journal had actually happened."

"So," M chimed in. "It's a hoax?"

"But the blood spots!" I said. "And the tear drops on the pages where the narrator talks about having betrayed his brother!"

The Librarian nodded. "It does seem to be quite a lot of effort to go to in order to produce such a forgery. Are we to think that the perpetrator not only cut himself open, but derived just the right way to splatter his blood across the pages? Perhaps it could be pig or cow blood, but still."

"And the way the hand gets more jittery and becomes incomprehensible..." I shook my head.

"There's more, though," the Librarian added, at which A, T, and M all raised an eyebrow. "Consider this. Just what kind of temple robber keeps a *journal*? That is probably the stupidest thing a temple robber could do. It would be a terrible liability. And how is it that the journal just happens to start only days before the terrifying encounter described at the shrine? The details he recounts all feed into the eventual discovery of the tainted shrine. It's all a little too carefully *constructed*."

A chimed in. "It's horrible, too, to think that someone invented such a grotesque fiction. And what would they gain from doing so? The perverse knowledge that they had filled other's minds with impious thoughts?"

"The writer of this journal showed us something important," the Librarian insisted. "It is why this journal remains in the Dark Archive and was not burned."

"Tiím went into the shrine," I said. "And the others didn't."

"We know that a melting simulacrum of him emerged from the shrine, but not that he himself truly did. If the narrator is right, and he and Ekil became trapped in some kind of Ahdez-above-ground, then it is possible that Tiím in fact survived and was redeemed for his act of self-sacrifice trying to save another." The Librarian inhaled and exhaled, seeming to collect his thoughts. "The status of this journal is uncertain. It could be genuine or a forgery. It could reveal that the gods are terrible and ruthless, or that human vice is far worse than anything the gods could inflict upon us. It could also reveal that human virtue can redeem us, or that no amount of virtue can redeem those with evil in their hearts and minds. Can man be 'the measure of all things?' To that I ask, 'which man, when, and in what capacity?' Man is a moving target, one whom, we hope, can better himself, become stronger, brighter, kinder, more knowledgable, more compassionate, and more intelligent. Man is certainly capable of the human horrors detailed in this journal. However, I do not want those qualities as having any part in the measure of all things."

The Librarian and the others left later that evening, and the Librarian took the journal with him. I never saw it again, nor did I relate its contents to any other living soul. I recall that I tried to go to bed immediately after seeing them out, but I stirred for some time, for my mind was roiling. I got up in the depths of night, lit a candle, and composed the outline and some initial notes for what would become *Our Responsibility to Others*.

It was an immediate success in the intellectual community of Sóf, and I found students flocking to me such as never before in my career. I managed, somehow, to build on that momentum and gain intellectual prestige as I have gotten older. I hope it is clear now why, as certain individuals have noted, I received those accolades with reticent smiles and "a kind of intense humility," to quote an orator I consider a friend, who was introducing me to a group in Apmonómen.

It is because I never solved the contradiction. I never escaped the quandary which led me to that work of the Dark Archive—if human perspective defines existence, then what of the gods? The Librarian and his journal didn't so much provide an answer as a way to live with the question's consequences. If the world contains irreconcilable questions and internally inconsistent data sets, how do we integrate, comprehend, and process our world regardless?

I am gone; as you read this, I am only words on a page. My work is left to the world, and the world must decide what to do with it. You now know the terrible thing, that jolt of energy that made it all possible, and how horrifying it was. If you condemn my entire work to oblivion on this basis, it is nothing for me, as I thought through these problems for the joy of thinking through problems with equally dedicated thinkers. You can condemn me as a heretic if you wish, for I am already dead. My concern remains only for those who were associated with me during my lifetime and their descendants.

Please though, if you do decide to condemn my work to the flames, do check the inscription just inside the frontis of each one. It is worth noting that I have dedicated every treatise, every theorum, every collection of my letters, to the gods, that I might have brought them greater glory through my all my deeds on earth.

Rite of Courage

Kele's mother took her to temple for the first time when she was eight years old. She had been to the community shrine with her mother many times prior, but the sight of the temple left her awestruck. Columns of marble and metallic tripods lined the pathways. The flowerbeds and shrubs had been ever so carefully pruned. Incense wafted, particulate strands gyrating and distending in the gentle breeze. Light shone down, spattering the ground through the leaves of enormous trees. The complex itself was expansive. Three marble patios surrounded an enclosed central chamber, all atop a hillside grove that must have been at least five hundred mettrs square.

The space itself seemed to be inhaling and exhaling with the ebb and flow of the wind. Kele's heart slowed and she let herself gaze up into the trees. She let the sounds of nature—the chirps of birds and the rustling of squirrels amongst the shrubs—pass over her, through her.

All at once, her foot hit something and she stumbled, tripping, barely righting herself before falling into a shrubbery. Coming out of her daze, she realized that she'd inadvertently wandered up against the edge of the pathway, and her foot had hit the row of bricks lining it.

"Kele," her mother called. "This way."

Kele hurried toward her mother, and they proceeded toward the central chamber.

More people appeared as they drew closer, not just other visitors like herself, her mother, and her fourteen-year-old cousin Hállok, but temple attendants, too. Those wore long, white robes that stopped only just above the ankles, and the tops were adorned with long hoods. And their forms… she couldn't see any of their faces, but the chests and hips… Kele was only eight, but she could tell that the attendants were unmistakably women. Thoughts of the trees and sculpted gardens left her. She had never before seen women doing anything that seemed important. Men ran the stalls in the market. Men built the buildings. Men smithed the bronze and iron. Men defended the walls of Fid. Women, Kele understood, were to stay at home and manage household affairs.

She trained her gaze on a group of priestesses, six in total, who had congregated around a particularly large nearby tripod. One priestess pulled down her hood. Her head had been shaved, but her features were unmistakably feminine. She reached into her pocket and retrieved a bag. She then reached inside the bag and pulled out a handful of powder, which she promptly threw into the tripod. It erupted into blue flames momentarily, followed by a plume of dark purple smoke. The priestess and the other five attendants began chanting words Kele didn't understand. The words drifted away as she followed Hállok and her mother past them.

At the center of the structure stood an enormous statue of the hermaphrodite god Isórrop, whose worldly manifestation was the white moon visible in the sky half a month at a time. Now that Kele was old enough, her mother had told her that morning, it was time for her to join Hállok and herself on their monthly trip to the shrine, to pray to the family deity for favorable treatment while he watched over them.

Kele approached the statue, still following her mother and watching her intently. Her calm had evaporated, replaced by the worry that she would inadvertently do something inappropriate. She watched her mother and Hállok kneel, then knelt herself. She watched them clasp their hands together, and she mimicked those movements, too. Then they closed their eyes, so she took a deep breath and closed her eyes, too.

At first, her mind raced with worries—how would she know when to open her eyes? What if her mother left her? No, her mother wouldn't do that. And she was in a temple of the god. Nowhere on earth could be safer. She realized then that the incense was stinging her nostrils, and she fought the reflex to rub at her nose. She had to remain still until her mother told her to open her eyes, and that was what she was going to do. She tried to focus on her breathing, but that only made the incense sting harder, and was it just her imagination, or were the words of the chanting priestess in the background getting louder? It must have been her imagination, except, was she catching bits of the speech? Yes, it was as though the words were just starting to make sense in fits and bursts. She focused all her attention on the intermittently comprehensible utterances.

"Eke melliu home is where assán assán muku terrible fear, but you will calm thesselé lommok tele oko. The god decrees it. You are his servant. The god names you his servant, Kele."

Her eyes burst open. Her mother was staring directly into her eyes.

"Kele?" her mother said.

Her mother's hand was on her shoulder. Hállok was kneeling in front of her also, a concerned expression on his face as well.

Kele gulped. "I'm sorry, mother."

"Are you alright?"

"Yes," she gulped and nodded. "I think it's just the incense."

"It can be a bit much the first time," Hállok said.

Her mother took Kele's hand in hers with a smile. "Let's go home."

As Kele walked back through the hall, she tried to focus on the words of the six priestesses at the enormous tripod once more, but what little she caught had become gibberish again. Just as they passed, the priestess leading the chant drew up her hood, and the six dispersed into the temple, presumably off to perform other duties.

Kele thought about the words she had heard the priestess speak for the rest of that day. She hurried through her chores, preoccupied. Her mother's voice seemed miles away as they prepared dinner together, and when her father and brothers came home, she found herself drifting away from the conversation about the events in the Fid marketplace and rolling those words over and over in her mind. If it really had been the voice of the god, he had called her his servant.

Should she tell someone? If she told anyone, it would be her mother. She focused her attention on her mother, who happened at that moment to be smiling at her father's story.

Fear held her back; intense fear. She was only eight, but she had already heard the stories of the ones who had defied the gods, the ones were guilty of the crime called impiety. The god Thenneto cast away the worst people, the ones who'd most misbehaved, to the place known as Ahdez, an underground realm where the worst souls were perpetually interred and denied the opportunity to be born anew. Kele knew that disrespecting the gods was even worse than disrespecting her parents. She didn't want to go to Ahdez, and so she decided then and there to keep her experience to herself.

"How was temple?" her brother Torrél asked.

"It was beautiful," Kele replied as quickly as she could.

"Eat all of your potatoes," Kele's mother instructed Torrél. Kele was glad for the diversion.

Later that night, Kele had a hard time drifting off to sleep. She kept thinking about the voice in her head, the strange, meaningless words suddenly becoming real words in her mind. Was Isórrop calling her to serve him? Would it be impiety not to follow his command? She wanted to cry, but she told herself not to. She would have to be strong. Mother was always saying that the men go on and on about the boys learning courage, but it was important for young women to be courageous, too.

Somehow, she eventually drifted off to slumber.

When she awoke the next morning, the events of the temple seemed a million mettrs away. She washed herself in the stream at the edge of their property with her brothers, came in and got dressed, and immediately set about her daily chores. Her life settled back into the daily routine she was accustomed to.

Isórrop continued climbing in the sky day after day, moving from the East slowly to the West, and finally disappearing behind the horizon a week and a half later. Atax and Stathro, the red moon and blue moon then danced across the sky, occasionally alone, occasionally together, until the first of the next month, which Kele found very suddenly upon her, a special day called Kens.

Kele's brothers had told her the old stories once. They had been trying to scare her, but she hadn't been scared, and she'd told them as much. (Okay, she'd been a little scared.)

Before the gods were really understood, people used to believe that the moons themselves were actually the gods, and not just their visages in the sky. They believed that every Kens, the day when none of the moons were present, was a day that the gods had abandoned the earth, and might never return again. If humans were bad on Kens, then the next day, Atax would burn everything, Stathro would flood everything, and Isórrop would carve out everyone's eyes, and chop off their ears, noses, and hands, so that no person could be certain of what they were seeing, hearing, or even feeling.

Okay, maybe she'd been more than just a little scared. But the point was that she'd told her brothers that she wasn't. And that also helped her understand why, even today, no one went outside on Kens, no one went to the market on Kens, no one trained on Kens, and no one certainly worked on Kens. She typically talked to her family and played games with them indoors, but she sometimes imagined ancient people hiding in caves, fearing to perform even the most minor tasks.

That month on Kens, Kele found her memory drifting back to her experience of understanding the priestesses' words, for the day following Kens would be Ozor, the day of Isórrop's return, and that would mean another trip to the temple. Her forgotten fear came rushing back. What would happen this time? Would the god speak to her again?

When she woke up on Ozor, she moved through her morning routine preoccupied with thoughts of what to do at the temple. What do you do when you think you're hearing the god speak to you? Could she ask her mother? She pondered spilling the whole story that morning. Her mother was putting the offerings together in a basket, and Kele had nearly worked up the courage to broach the subject when Hállock announced his arrival from the entrance chamber of their home.

"Go see if he's brought Aunt Reanna's gooseberries and cinnamon, would you, Kele?" her mother asked, and the moment was lost. Kele ran off to do as she was told.

Just like last month, they walked together down the streets into the big city of Fid, which felt so busy and boisterous to Kele. Her brother Torrél had told her that Fid was nothing compared to mainland cities like Zotik,

Stheno, and Épanngel. She couldn't even imagine what bigger and noisier than Fid might look like.

They approached the large hill and began their climb, the busy streets receding beneath them, trees and grass returning to the streetside, the street eventually becoming a path, and the path leading up to large, marble gates.

All the awe and wonder of Kele's first visit was gone. Apprehension had replaced it. She walked delicately, as though her feet might break the path. She dared not look at anyone or anything other than her mother and cousin. She followed them with her eyes fixed on what was in front of her. She ignored the attendants as they entered the central chamber. She tried to push the incense smell out of her nostrils. She didn't want any more confusing messages from the god. She just wanted to live in peace.

They reached the statue of Isórrop, and her mother knelt, setting the basket of offerings down before her. Kele knelt, too, clasped her hands together, and closed her eyes.

She tried to fill her head with her own words, her own thoughts, mentally shouting to herself anything that came to mind, thoughts about her family, about their market stall, about her brothers, but the voices of the priestess managed to slip through: "Eke illo kezemmnaos mill mekka pe. Ezna Isórrop mai kenne ou menzanéllpiu. Jummí nan eke illo, kon venma sa."

She took deep breaths, and continued listening, but

the words remained unintelligible. She allowed herself a bit of a smile as the priestess's voice continued, and still, Kele could not understand a word. She dared not call out; she dared not move. But if she could have, she would have jumped up and let out a shout of pure joy. Nothing the priestess was saying was making sense!

A roar, deep, guttural, and masculine, interrupted her reverie. Gasps and shouts followed it. Kele's eyes burst open, and she swiveled in the direction of the sounds. A man stood, a quarter way around the statue, not ten mettrs away, holding a knife outstretched in his hand. His eyes looked red, and sweat dripped in beads down his face.

"I'll do it!" he shouted. "I swear I will!"

Kele felt her mother grab her and pull her close, while Hállok stepped in front of them both. Kele craned her neck around her to see the man, who was now swinging the knife about, slicing through the air in wide, crazed arcs. Others were shouting now, and some were running from the shine.

"Stay perfectly still," her mother said. "Both of you."

Out of the side of her vision, Kele noticed a movement that was not jolting or twitching, but calm and methodical. White, shimmering robes moved in along her peripheral vision, forming into a wave of attendants, who effervesced toward the man with the knife, seeming to glide on their feet.

All at once, they formed a semi-circle around him. The woman at the center pulled down her hood and revealed herself to be the same priestess that Kele had seen the month before, the one who's speech had changed.

"Kamen," the priestess said, in a calm level voice. "What is the matter?"

Tears welled up in the man's eyes. "It's all death!" he roared. "Death, death, death! I want it over!"

The priestess nodded. "You're in so much pain, Kamen. But please stop. Especially in Isórrop's presence. The god desires balance above all things, harmony."

The man's eyes grew redder, and he took a step forward toward the priestess, his knife outstretched at her, though wobbling in his hand. "Where's— my— harmony!" he roared, spittle flying from his mouth. "Where!" A demand, not a question.

The priestess did not flinch. "Your pain is real, Kamen. No one denies that. In our limited perspectives as mortals, we cannot always understand why things are as they are. That is natural."

"No!" He roared, and lunged toward the priestess. Gasps and shrieks went up from the nearby congregants, but the priestess wheeled, dodging the knife. The other attendants moved out his way, and he stumbled past them all, falling, the knife flying out of his hand.

Hállok ran forward, and Kele's mother let out a yelp. He grabbed up the knife, then scampered toward Kele and her mother.

Kamen remained sprawled on the floor, sobbing and groaning. The attendants moved toward him, laying hands on his back.

The head priestess strode up to Kele, her mother, and Hállok. Kele looked up into her sharp eyes, wondering at the powers of this awesome figure before her.

"Thank you, young man," the priestess said, and then turned to Kele's mother. "What is his name?"

"His name is Hállok, your grace," mother said, her hands clasping Kele's side ever so tightly.

"Hállok," the priestess said, "I will need to take that weapon. It must be destroyed."

Hállok held the thing out like a piece of rotten meat. The priestess took a cloth from a pocket in her robes, and took the knife in the cloth, being careful not to touch it herself.

The priestess turned her attention to mother. "He must perform the purification ritual before returning to the shrine."

"He will, your grace."

The priestess nodded and retreated.

Hállok and Kele's mother shared a look. Kele thought that Hállok looked indignant, while her mother looked upset.

The trio retreated from the temple in silence.

Kele's mother spent the entire trip home haranguing Hállok: "Didn't I tell you to stay put?" ("Yes.") "What if the priestess had thought that you had wanted to attack someone, too?" ("She didn't.") "Now you'll have to do the purification ritual. You know what kind of people usually have to do that, right?" ("Yes, I know.")

Kele largely pushed the conversation mentally aside and thought of the priestess. Everything about her fascinated Kele—the way she and the others had walked so confidently, effortlessly toward Kamen, the way she had spoken so calmly, even compassionately, to someone so threatening, the way she had dodged his attack with ease, the way she seemed to emit an aura of respect, of reverence for everything around her, even foolish, angry men like Kamen, who were so—Kele hesitated to think it, but there it was—beneath her.

The priestess wouldn't think such things, Kele told herself.

"Are you going to train, and help you father at market, and purify yourself tomorrow, young man?" Her mother was still at it.

"I dunno." Hállok's voice was growing irritated. "Probably."

"The purification ritual takes three hours. Did you know that?"

"No. I didn't. Thank you for letting me know, Aunt Mara. I'll find a way."

Kele's mother finally seemed to register the fact that Hállok was shutting her out. "I'm sorry, Hállok. That was very brave. But you need to consider how your behaviors will be interpreted by others. I'm just worried about your reputation in the community, is all."

"Thank you, Aunt Mara," Hállok mumbled, seeming unconvinced.

They remained silent until they reached Kele's home, where Hállok said goodbye and ran off toward Kele's uncle's house, further down the street.

Kele's mother did the remainder of the daily chores in silence, and Kele did not dare break it. Kele noticed her mother seemed nervous. Kele wondered if she was just imagining things as she watched her mother do the washing, but by the time they were preparing dinner, Kele could tell she had been right from the way her mother chopped the vegetables.

It was when her father and brothers walked through the door, and Kele saw her mother descend carefully into her seat at the table that Kele knew what was bothering her mother. She would have to tell Kele's father about what had happened.

To Kele's surprise, he handled it well. He just shook his head, and twisted his lips. "That Hállok. You gave him a good talking to?"

"I did," Kele's mother replied.

"I should have a talk with his father, too." He looked at Kele. "And you, Kele?"

"I was fine."

"It must have been frightening."

Kele wanted to reply that she had been afraid, but

she'd seen the priestesses, and she wanted to be like them. She wanted to have the courage to defuse any situation with words, and to know that she was capable of repelling any attack. But she couldn't say such things to her father. "I wasn't too frightened."

Her father nodded. "Who did you say this man was?"

"The priestess called him Kamen," Kele's mother said.

"Ah." Her father nodded knowingly. "I think I told you about him. Remember two years ago, I mentioned that a smithy suddenly stopped showing up for clothes for his kids?"

"Oh my," Kele's mother said.

Kele remembered that story, too. He and his whole family had contracted an illness. He'd ruined himself financially paying the doctors, and in the end, only he had survived, while his wife and two sons had both perished. No wonder he'd been so sad.

"We should say a prayer for him tonight," her father suggested. Everyone around the table nodded.

The family gathered around their small house shrine that night, and her father led the prayer for Kamen. Afterward, her father and the boys went upstairs, but Kele followed her mother into the kitchen.

"Would you like some tea?" her mother asked, putting a small cauldron over the embers.

Kele nodded.

"What an eventful day for you," she said. "Tell me, were you really not that frightened?"

Kele hesitated. "I think... I think I wasn't. I was watching the priestesses. They're amazing."

Her mother nodded. "They train like the men do. Well, almost like the men do. They learn even more, it's said."

"More?" Kele raised an eyebrow.

Her mother let out a small sigh. "How to explain? Men learn a certain kind of speech. How to debate. How to make an argument. How to... well, it's like wrestling, but verbal."

Kele laughed. She'd seen her brothers wrestling. Perhaps it was just that they weren't that good at it yet.

Her mother continued. "The priestesses learn how to calm people with words. How to heal with words."

"Not all their words make sense," Kele said. She realized the implications of her statement only after it had left her lips.

Her mother nodded. "That's Léks, the way people talked a long, long time ago. Those are the old chants to the moons you heard. They go back hundreds of years. Maybe more."

Kele looked at the empty doorway, just to make sure, then turned back to her mother. "Have you ever... heard of someone understanding Léks?"

"You mean..." Her mother paused, looking at her sternly for many moments. "Have you understood some of what the priestesses were saying in Léks?"

Kele nodded meekly.

Her mother nodded slowly, a blank look on her face.

"Am I in trouble?" Kele asked.

Her mother let out a small, startled breath, then smiled, and said, "No, darling, you're not in trouble."

"But, what does it mean that I—"

"It means," her mother said with a wry smile, "that if you wanted to, and if they accept you, you could be one of Isórrop's priestesses yourself."

When Kele woke the next morning, she entertained the notion that her discussion with her mother had been a dream. Perhaps she had gone to bed after the prayer, and their discussion of the priestesses afterward had been an invention of her overactive imagination.

At first, this story was easy enough to maintain. She bathed with her brothers in the stream as normal, dressed as normal, and had breakfast with her family as normal. However, after breakfast, as the boys were preparing to go with their father and Kele was preparing the dishes in the kitchen, she noticed her mother pull her father aside and have a hushed conversation with him, one which continued for multiple minutes, and seemed to grow more and more tense.

Eventually, her father seemed to concede to whatever it was her mother had said. He then called out for Kele's brothers, and the men promptly left.

Kele decided not to ask.

The rest of the day proceeded ordinarily, and she soon forgot the morning incident. She didn't think of it again until her father returned home, and she watched as he handed over to her mother a parcel about the width and depth of a cutting board, and about three times as thick. Her mother placed the parcel on the high shelf above the pantry doors, and dinner proceeded as usual.

Her brothers didn't ask about it, meaning her father had already told them what it was—or perhaps he'd refused to tell them what it was. Either way, they didn't feel the need to talk about it around her.

They talked about all the usual things at dinner. One of the new styles of robes was selling particularly well; some of the other stall owners were getting upset over the rising price of space rental that the city council had enacted; and so on. Kele ate her food quietly, occasionally glancing at the wooden box atop the pantry.

After dinner, her father corralled her brothers up the stairs, and Kele and her mother stayed in the kitchen and cleared the dishes as usual. Instead of washing them right away, however, her mother told her to sit at the table. She removed the parcel from the top of the pantry, set it on the table and unwrapped its paper exterior in front of them both. Beneath the wrapping lay a very plain wooden box. Kele's mother pulled open the lid. Inside, Kele discovered twelve scrolls bound in pure white ribbon.

Kele gulped. "What are these?"

Her mother pointed to the first scroll from the left. "This one will teach you how to read." Then the next two. "And these are from a writer called Hossád."

"Father has talked about him, right? He wrote about how to run a market stall."

"Yes, and about many other things. To you, he will teach about the gods. All of them."

Kele looked up at her mother. "Will I be a priestess when I've read all of these?" It seemed a bit too simple.

"No. If you can learn to read, and if you can do it quickly and well, then we take you to the shrine for further study. But we're a ways off from that."

"Do all of the priestesses study?"

"Yes."

It was then that Kele noticed tears at the edges of her mother's eyes. "Mother, what's—?"

"It's nothing," her mother said, shaking her head, smiling, and quickly regaining her composure. She paused a moment, lost in thought, then her smile flattened, and she began speaking softly. "If the temple will take you... then you will begin living there... very soon. You should know that."

"But I could come visit, right?"

Her mother nodded slowly. "Yes." But it did not sound like a very convincing word to Kele's ears. "Don't worry," her mother added. "Priestesses families are treated with great respect. If it does happen, it will be an honor. And if it doesn't, there will be no shame. There is honor enough just in trying."

Kele worked on the first scroll with her mother that night. She went over the alphabet dozens of times, trying to match the letters to the sounds. She even managed to sound out Hossád's first few sentences, but she was soon exhausted, and her mother sent her to bed.

She looked at her mother putting away the parcel as she left the kitchen, noticing how odd it was that for the first time in her life she was seeing her mother simultaneously happy and sad. It was the first moment she was not really sure whether or not she wanted to become a priestess after all.

The next day, Kele found herself exempted from all of her usual chores. Her mother sat her down at the kitchen table with the box of scrolls and instructed her to continue. When Kele tired of sounding out the words of Hossád's first scroll, she unrolled another.

Around lunchtime, she began to grow weary of the reading, and her head felt weighted down by all the new information. She decided to simply go over the letters of the alphabet again, and, finding them easier to remember than the night before, gained a sense of accomplishment—she was learning.

In the early afternoon, her mother did interrupt her to help prepare for dinner, and the scrolls were packed up and put away. All throughout the preparation, though, all Kele could think about was how Atax had made the land, Stathro the seas, and Isórrop all the plants, animals, and people. She'd read only two scrolls and she yearned to read the other ten.

Over the next week and a half, she did just that. She used the following week review all of the scrolls again, from start to finish.

It was around this time that she noticed her father and brothers were treating her differently. With her brothers, it was obvious—they weren't teasing her anymore. With her father, she couldn't place it exactly, but the way he talked to her was different. He didn't give her commands anymore, as he might have done in the past. Instead, he would look at her mother, and her mother would ask her to do something instead.

Before Kele knew it, it was Kens again, the day of rest, and then came the day that she had been anticipating, her next visit to the temple.

That morning, only her brother Torrél went off with her father, and her brother Zekne stayed behind.

"Hállok isn't coming with us?" Kele asked.

"No," her mother said. "It wouldn't be appropriate today. Not after what happened."

"But... I thought he performed the purification ritual, like you told him to."

Her mother shook her head. "He did, but... today is a very important day."

All three dressed in their best clothes, and her

mother prepared a particularly large basket of offerings. At this, Kele felt a pang of shame. She didn't want her family to eat less because of her. But then she remembered what her mother had said the month prior: the families of priestesses were treated well. If Kele could become a priestess, her family would be all right. Better than all right.

They left earlier than usual and walked quickly through the city. Just before they passed through the marble gates, Kele caught a glimpse of Zekne smiling at her, but he quickly averted his eyes and pretended he wasn't.

Kele's heart raced, and her heart filled with an entirely new kind of fear, the dread of anticipation.

Instead of walking directly in and approaching Isórrop's shrine, the three of them skirted the central complex, and entered a clearing amongst the trees behind it.

Four hooded figures stood about a large rock. One of them removed her hood as Kele, her mother, and her brother approached.

"Your grace," her mother clasped her forearms together and bowed. The priestess merely clasped her forearms together. Kele looked up at her mother—tears streamed from her eyes. Zekne's face was pinched.

The priestess turned her attention to Kele, gazing down at her. "Name the gods. All of them."

Kele gulped, and named them all, in Hossád's order. She skipped one, then remembered she'd skipped it, and began again from that place. Otherwise, she thought she'd gotten them all.

"The names of the letters of Léks."

Kele listed those, too.

"What does Isórrop desire most?"

"Balance," Kele replied immediately.

"A priestess must devote her whole life to the god. Is that what you want?"

Kele gulped. She dared a glance at her mother's red face, her proud smile, how she still was unable to hold back her tears.

Kele looked back at the priestess. "Yes."

"Am I a priestess now?" Kele asked the priestess after her mother and brother Zekne had left.

"No," the priestess responded. "You have much training to do before you will be a priestess. This is only the beginning of your journey."

What followed were days and days of quiet study.

Kele was given a straw mat in a side room of the temple, a room she shared with five other priestess, the youngest of whom was at least two years older than her. Her first night she'd felt terribly, terribly lonely; she'd even prayed to awaken at home in her bed the next morning, but the next day had begun, and she'd been given much more to read, and she immersed herself in the scrolls.

On the eighteenth of that first month, the day before

Kens, she finished her evening lessons and expected to join the other priestesses for evening meal, but was instead lead by her instructor into the main complex where she found her mother and both brothers waiting for her.

"You will spend Kens with your family," the priestess said. "And then return here for morning prayer on Ozor. Understood?"

"Yes, your grace." Kele bowed, then took off toward her smiling mother and siblings.

Her studies proceeded in much the same way for a full year. She would spend the whole month reading scrolls at the temple and eating simple food, returning home every eighteenth for a single day with her family.

A year into her training, the exercises changed abruptly. One morning, the head priestess informed her that, from then on, she would be doing physical training in the mornings and study only in the afternoons. Two other young priestesses led her into the grove where she'd been initiated. They doffed their robes and taught her various stretches and movements, such as lunges and stances. Later they taught her whole sequences of movements.

Two months later, she joined a large group of priestesses in a field much further back in the temple complex, and all of them performed the exercises together. Before long, Kele realized she was learning the rudiments of self-defense: block, dodge, parry, disarm, spin, and so on.

Her training passed in this way for many years. She

turned nine, then ten, then eleven, then twelve. One day, just after her twelfth birthday, she discovered on one of her visits home that her brother Torrél had rented a market stall of his own and was expanding the family business to include foodstuffs in addition to textiles and housewares.

Her physical education remained fairly constant throughout this time, but her studies changed yet again. As usual, an older priestess gave her a scroll. As usual, she read it. And, as usual, the older priestess asked her questions to ensure that Kele had understood what she'd read. Kele answered all those questions with ease, as she usually did, and was prepared to move on to the next scroll, when, out of the blue, the older priestess asked, "what is important about this story?"

Kele blinked. She'd never been asked such a question before. "Well, the god Isórrop grew angry with their son Pollem and their daughter Tress, and so he cast them out—"

"What does his anger *mean*?"

Kele blinked. "They violated his law. Siblings should not lie together. He was angry."

"Why is his law important?"

Kele felt wholly uncomfortable at this question. It wasn't her place to judge to the worth of the god's laws.

"He's a god."

"And his children were other gods. In the story, why should his law be important to them?"

The awkward questions proceeded, and Kele did her best to answer, but at the end she felt she'd disappointed her instructor. She lay on her straw mat that night wondering whether or not she'd made a mistake in trying to become a priestess.

The next day the strange questions continued, and the next.

The day after that, Kele sighed, and blurted out, "I don't want to question the gods, your grace!"

The older priestess smiled and nodded. "We are not questioning the gods, Kele. We are understanding them. We must know their motivations, their thoughts, the reasons why they do what they do. We must understand it all. Not just *what* happens in the tales, but *why* those events happened."

Kele shook her head. "I don't understand."

"Have you seen," the priestess nodded toward the center of the shrine, "when men show up dressed in regal clothes, and the head priestess and all the high priestesses will go off with them?"

Kele nodded. Such events happened perhaps once or twice a week.

"They ask us for advice."

Kele's eyes went wide. *Men* asking *women* for advice?

"As the servants of the gods, it is presumed that we know the best course of action in difficult matters. And of course, they want to be seen as knowing all the answers themselves, so they must be discrete."

"We tell them what to do?"

"Not exactly. We suggest. But it is enough. These suggestions can impact business, trade, courts..." the priestess paused and pursed her lips. "Even war," she whispered. "It is very, *very* important that we understand the gods' intent as best we can."

Kele nodded.

That night she lay awake, staring at the dark ceiling. The vague shimmer of fire light from somewhere out beyond her room danced across it. It was years, likely even decades, before she would be asked to join such discussions, let alone weigh in. But... there it was. It would be her responsibility to advice noble, powerful men on their most perplexing problems. Matters of state, matters of legality, matters of life and death. Could she do that?

She didn't know.

Still, she persisted. This new discovery made her want to interpret the will of the gods all that much fervently. She read voraciously. If she would one day have to advise politicians and generals on the best course of action, she would provide them only the best opinions, and that meant learning all she could now.

Her physical and mental training proceeded apace, and she found the months passing by ever more rapidly. At home, while Torrél continued to expand the family business in the marketplace, Zekne turned fourteen and decided to enlist.

Once, just after Kele had turned seventeen, Zekne came home dressed in armor and carrying about twice the muscle she remembered him having. Her father surveyed the table at dinner, smiling. "A protégé, a warrior, and a priestess. Each one of you has made me so proud."

Shortly after this event, Kele was told that she was approaching the point of gaining the status of full priestess, at which point she would be expected to take up full residence at Isórrop's shrine and no longer spend Kens with her family.

Just three months later, she undertook the rite of full initiation, and officially joined the priesthood of Isórrop. The high priestess herself shaved Kele's head in the sacred grove and gave her new robes, these embroidered with strands of silver that shimmered in the sun.

During the first year after her initiation, Kele felt she'd comfortably transitioned into her position, and she began to gain some confidence in her abilities. She even asked to be assigned to an initiate at the next available opportunity, so that she could help someone else along the way that she'd been helped.

A month after her eighteenth birthday, Kele awoke to an odd scuttling sound. Consciousness crept slowly back to her, and with a jolt, she realized that their room was pitch black, which it never should have been. A shuffling sound emanated from the hallway, and then a whisper of a voice—a *male* voice.

Kele tried to scream, but found she couldn't.

She scrambled up to her feet and shook the nearest priestess awake. She found her voice, finally, belatedly, and let out a shrieking roar.

Footsteps scrambled away, followed by the sound of many metallic objects jostling together. By the time the entire temple had been roused, the thieves had fled, taking with them many priceless relics. The temple guards who'd been up on duty were found unconscious by the fire in the main hall—drugged.

The next day, a well-dressed man showed up at the shrine for a consultation with all temple leaders. Kele suspected this time it was not for advice.

"Will the guards be okay?" Kele asked her mentor while they were studying the scrolls.

"Those were powerful drugs, but in time, yes."

"Will we ever get those relics back?"

"Perhaps." Her mentor shook her head. "It's unlikely."

Kele looked back and forth, checking if anyone else was nearby. The nearest other priestess was on the other side of the room. "Once, before I became a priestess, there was a man who drew a knife in the temple. Do you remember that?"

Her mentor nodded. "Yes, I think so. You were there for that?"

"I was. He attacked the high priestess, and she just... dodged, parried, redirected... We practice it every day, but I wonder if I could do it in the moment like that.

Last night I tried to scream, and my voice wouldn't come out. Perhaps, if I had been able to shout sooner, they wouldn't have gotten away..." She felt even more shame saying the words aloud.

"Nothing that happened last night was your fault, Kele."

Kele remained silent, not feeling the least bit absolved.

"The head priestess is the head priestess because she's faced so many situations like that in the past. She didn't get them all perfectly right the first time, either. She had to learn just like the rest of us."

Kele nodded, wondering when and how she would ever learn to handle such dangerous confrontations.

The two years following the break-in passed uneventfully. The two drugged guards did recover, and the temple hired four more guards, bringing the total to twelve. Meanwhile, Fid's pious carpenters and smithies supplied the temple with a steady stream of newly crafted religious icons.

Kele got assigned an initiate, Nikí, a shy girl of nine, and Kele delighted in teaching her the foundational scrolls and drawing her out of her self-imposed shell. She found that helping someone else gain confidence was incredibly helpful in bolstering her own.

Four months after Kele's twentieth birthday, a contingent of a dozen men showed up at the temple wearing robes of a make she'd never seen before. The head priestess and high priestesses gave them an audience, and the entire group disappeared into the woods behind the temple complex.

The time for evening meal came and went, and still, the temple leadership remained in the forest. The eldest journeywoman priestesses cast one another concerned looks. Everyone seemed worried about potential misdeeds at the hands of these strangers, but no one could muster the courage to interrupt them, either. Certainly no one could think of preparing food.

Just when the tension had begun to grow unbearable, the temple leadership and the foreigners returned to the shrine proper, the foreigners departing immediately, while the head priestess called everyone together in front of the statue of Isórrop.

"Those were delegates from Akhtm," the head priestess announced.

Murmuring erupted from the assembled attendants.

"That's in the north, right?" Kele whispered to her mentor. "The farthest north?"

Her mentor nodded.

The head priestess continued. "Akhtm has announced a discovery. Not only are there peoples beyond the great desert to the north, they are 'un-savage,' so to speak. They have writing, they have leaders, and they recognize the gods, albeit somewhat differently from us. It has been suggested that some may even understand the gods better than we do. They have evidence of cities that destroyed themselves because they did not achieve the correct *balance*. This is obviously of great interest to us.

"The Akhtmites wish to establish military, economic, and religious relations with the other cities of Palipolí, including Fid. They wish to invite a religious delegation to their city for a period of three years, to help them interpret these new findings and discover if these beliefs really are holy, or if they have in fact misunderstood the gods."

"Why are they inviting a delegation *now*?" This came from one of the eldest of the journeywoman priestesses. Everyone knew that Akhtm liked to send out their emissaries to other cities but remained unwelcoming to foreigners themselves.

"Akhtm has uncovered something else. Beyond the desert to the north, and beyond the peoples east of that desert, there is a city. It is perhaps the largest city on earth, and the rulers of that city rule over all other cities for hundreds of thousands of mettrs in all directions. They call this great city Seppóla, and its army..." The head priestess took a breath. "Its army is said to comprise over one hundred thousand soldiers."

A gasp went up from multiple priestesses. Even militaristic Épanngel only commanded an army of eight thousand soldiers.

"Akhtm wishes to create alliances," the head priestess said. "These people of Seppóla, who call themselves

Ksezians, if their army were to march on Palípoli, only an alliance of all our cities would ensure our survival. In return for access to their shrines and libraries, the Akhtmites wish for military support, as they would find themselves at the front line of any such invasion force."

The assembled priestesses began murmuring to one another.

"Ksezians?" Kele asked her mentor. "Does that even sound real? What do you think?"

"When I was younger, my father brought home stories of Akhtm explorers who'd found ruined cities in the northern deserts. He never mentioned people, though. I suppose it's possible."

The head priestess raised her hand, and the shrine went silent. "I will be selecting three priestesses for the three year delegation. The participants will be accompanied at all times by Fid soldiers and diplomats. Two temple guards will be selected as well, to ensure our priestesses' safety. Are there any further questions?"

The shrine remained silent.

"Good," the head priestess said. "Now let's get our evening meal started."

Somehow, Kele knew she would be selected. It did not surprise her in the least the next day when the head priestess made the announcement at morning meal. Kele would join Uneke, a priestess a few years older than herself, who she didn't know very well, and Alíza, one of the high priestesses, on the three year delegation to Akhtm.

Each of them was permitted one day at home with their families before they were to leave, with the date set for the second of the next month, less than a week away.

Kele caught her mentor grinning at her.

"What?" Kele asked.

"Nothing," her mentor said. Then, affecting a mock-seriousness, she added, "it would be highly inappropriate for a priestess of Isórrop to experience jealousy after all. Though seriously, I hope you enjoy this trip. And copy some scrolls for me while you're there, will you? Their libraries and shrines are supposed to rival Sóf's."

"I will," Kele replied. The full gravity of her mission hadn't really sunk in yet, but as the subsequent days went by, she began to wonder just how important the priestesses' role in the delegation really was. Akhtm wanted a military treaty, so the soldiers were necessary. And the diplomats were there to broker a fair deal. But were the priestesses any more than a gesture? Sure, they would read and copy scrolls, and evaluate these foreign claims on the gods. It didn't seem like she and her sisters were crucial elements. However, as a representative of Fid, she would do her best, even if her only job was to study.

Her father and mother both beamed with pride when she told them. Even Torrél smiled and congratulated her. They all promised to tell Zekne the next time he was off duty.

The next week was a flurry of preparations. Kele, Uneke, and Alíza were assigned a large chest, which was to hold all the possessions the three of them would require. The first inside were huge, newly-pressed slabs of endik paper, bottles of ink, and a box of quills. Next were two back-up robes for each of them. After that, they began to consider what gifts they might bring to their hosts, and they sent one of the younger temple guards on a mission into the city with a list of delicacies and Fid-specific finery to acquire.

On the day of their departure, two temple guards picked up the chest, and Kele, Uneke, and Alíza followed them down the hill to the city plaza, where they met three soldiers and three diplomats. They exchanged greetings, and then headed toward the port.

Kele had been impressed by the rush and bustle of the city her whole life, but the port even more so now. Men rushed about, moving crates, lifting things, hauling things in carts, shouting to one another. She found it unnerving, though the rest of her entourage seemed fine. Kele stayed close to her sisters, following wherever the group took them.

They reached the water, and Kele found herself gazing up at a tall ship, the top deck many heads higher than her own. It was built of a dark brown wood that reminded her of the venaát trees in the temple grove—she felt a sharp pang of desire for the safety and normalcy of the temple, which had been her home for almost twelve years. But her group moved up the gangplank, Kele focused her attention on remaining in formation, and the moment passed.

Atop the deck, the temple guards diverged from the rest of the delegation, hauling the large chest down a porthole and into the ship. Alíza, Uneke, and Kele followed after them. The hallways of the ship were cramped and narrow, and had the tendency to jostle this way and that. She would have an experience to share with Zekne, she thought, as she struggled to manage her footing in the shifting hallway. And now, she realized, the most uncomfortable feeling was forming in her head, growing worse every time the ship swayed.

They came to a door, which opened into a tiny room, its only furnishings being three wooden palettes buit into the wall of the ship—their beds.

The guards set the chest down in the corner of the cabin.

The older of the two turned to Alíza. "We'll take turns at your door."

"Thank you," Alíza said with a smile and shut the door behind them in the swaying room. She turned to Kele and Uneke. "How are you doing?"

"I'm fine," Uneke said. "I was actually at sea once, with my family."

"I actually feel a bit sick," Kele admitted.

Alíza nodded. "That is perfectly normal. If you feel very ill, take one of the guards with you up to the deck.

It's nothing to be ashamed of. If it happens frequently, there is a root you can chew."

Kele nodded.

Alíza proceeded on about their mission, and its importance, and which scrolls they were to attempt to read, but the more she talked, the more nauseous Kele began to feel, until—

"Sister?" Kele blurted out.

"Yes?"

"I need to go... now."

Alíza quickly side-stepped and pulled the cabin door open. Kele rushed out, only barely cognizant of the temple guard following in her wake. Back up the ladder, to the railing, and over it went everything she'd eaten for lunch.

She swiveled and reclined, letting her back slide down the railing post.

"Take deep breaths, slowly," the temple guard advised, and she did just that. Even though the boat was still swaying in the dock, she felt a bit better.

An angry shout from the dock below caught Kele's attention. She and the guard both peered out over the railing. Up the gangplank walked a group of people. Kele did not recognize their robes—they were neither of Fid nor Akhtm.

Four of them wore armor and carried swords. Another was unarmed, but his robes were intricately sewn and patterned—but dirty. It was an odd juxtaposition, a noble with dirty clothes... a noble on the run? A noble in disgrace? He held another man at the shoulder, another also wearing fancy, dirty robes. His eyes held a wildness, and a kind of detachment, and his hands were bound behind his back.

The six of them walked up the gangplank, the noble with free hands saying something to the guards, which Kele couldn't hear from this distance.

"Do you know what kind of robes those are?" Kele asked her guard.

"No, your grace," the guard said. "We should go back to the cabin, if your grace is feeling better."

The group of four soldiers and the two nobles climbed on board the deck, and immediately descended into the ship via a ladder on the other side of the deck.

Kele pulled herself up off the deck, and she, too, descended into the ship.

Kele felt a bit better after her first bout of nausea, but when the ship left port and became fully subjected to the rocking of the seas, she became ill twice more in quick succession. Alíza produced the root, some scraggly, bulbous thing, tore off a piece of it, and thrust it toward Kele. Although the last thing Kele wanted at that point was to put anything near her stomach, she stuffed the root in her mouth and chewed.

Just moments later, the quavering, sloshing feeling in her head diminished, although her eyelids grew heavy, and her senses dulled, too. "Thank you," she said to her sister, though her voice was still hoarse.

"We have plenty more." Alíza shifted herself so as to include Uneke in the conversation, too. Uneke, who had been sitting on a palette reading a scroll, looked up.

"In addition to nausea, there is another malady we much manage on this voyage. It is called 'cabin fever.' We are going to be in this room together for over two weeks. I know that doesn't sound like a long time, but trust me, you will tire of these walls. The temple guards will bring us our meals, and we can go up onto the deck for only two hours per day. We must make the most of those. And above all, I have strict instructions for us to avoid contact with the crew and any other passengers not part of the delegation."

Uneke quirked her head. "Why?"

"For our safety. As long as we stay within vicinity of our temple guards at all times, I'm sure everything will be fine."

There was silence for several moments. Uneke seemed to be debating whether or not to press her line of questioning. Kele was simply happy to be feeling better. In the end, Uneke simply asked, "anything else?"

"No," Alíza said, taking a seat on her own palette.

Kele scrambled up to her own palette, lay down, and closed her eyes. Perhaps the root would help her sleep through the voyage. Funny to think that her greatest enemy aboard the ship would be her own boredom.

—

The first three days of the voyage passed uneventfully. Kele took the root at regular intervals throughout her first day, but on the second, Alíza advised her to take a break from it, and see if her nausea returned. Thankfully, it didn't.

Over the course of the second day, her perceptions became lucid again, and she decided to at least get some reading in. She pored over scrolls when the sun was up, and lay silently when it was dark. The guards brought the priestesses three meager meals a day, and she was often hungry, but she did not complain. Uneke gobbled down her small portions and was moody afterward, but she, too, said nothing.

Twice a day, the three of them and their guards went up onto the deck of the ship. They arrived just as the bulk of the crew was heading down below deck. Some of them would turn and look at the priestesses. Kele didn't like the way they looked at her, their eyes frighteningly covetous and filled with violence. She admitted to herself, and had been aware for some years now, that there was something fascinating about men, and there was something of that in this, but her overwhelming response to them was revulsion and mostly fear. She was glad to find the temple guards at her side, and the crew shuffling down below deck.

A few of the crew remained on the deck during these times, usually the captain and another man who, like the captain, wore nicer clothes than the rest. A couple of others would tend the masts and not pay them any mind.

The priestesses would walk in circles around the deck on these all-too-brief excursions. Kele's legs felt stiff and sore at first, and only just after she'd loosened up a bit, it would be time to go back to their quarters.

During one such walk on the fourth day of their voyage, Kele remarked that the captain was absent. Only the well-dressed man, who normally accompanied him, stood upon the platform at the center of the deck, which Kele had learned was called the helm.

"The captain's not here today," Kele said to Alíza. "He's been here every other time."

Alíza nodded. "Perhaps he's busy today."

That seemed reasonable, but when they returned again to the deck for their evening stroll, the captain was still absent, and the well-dressed man was missing, too. Another man, one of the regular crew, stood at the helm instead.

Alíza pulled one of the temple guards aside, while Kele and Uneke both stood and watched the silent conversation, or rather, a silent assortment of orders Alíza appeared to be giving the guard. He himself remained silent throughout and simply nodded at the end.

"What is going on?" Uneke said, when Alíza returned.

"I don't yet know," Alíza said. "But I will."

That night strange sounds found their way into

Kele's ears. Muffled cries and pained moans punctuated her fitful sleep.

She found she could not sleep, and, feeling again slightly queazy from the rocking of the boat, pulled herself off her palette and went to the chest to get more of the root.

Just as she'd stuffed some of the bitter plant in her mouth, she heard a moan from directly behind her and froze, pierced with terror. Another small moan, in the female register. Kele found the will to turn herself around. She crept toward the center of the room, and under the cyan light of Isórrop and Stathro both, Kele could just make out shudders and jerky movements of limbs from Alíza's palette. Alíza let out another pained whine, and Kele rushed to her side.

Kele put her hand on Alíza's forehead, which was wet with sweat and warm to the touch.

"Alíza?" Kele asked. "Alíza, can you hear me?"

She got only another moan in reply, and Alíza jerked her whole body around to lie on her other side, then moaned again.

Kele roused Uneke, who marched to the door.

"Alíza is very ill—"

Kele noticed it, too. It was very dark in the hallway, but even in the dim light of of the moons, it was clear that the guard's skin was flushed red and sweat was pouring down of him, pooling on the floor. His legs were wobbling and he was using the wall for support. It looked as though it was taking all of his energy to merely remain standing.

"You have to lie down!" Kele stepped into the hall.

"I cannot... leave the priestesses unprotected..." he muttered.

"Then we'll rouse the other guard," Uneke said. "Take us to him."

The guard led them down the hallway, leaning into the wall, and they came to another room similar to their own. A moan emanated from somewhere else on the ship, perhaps above them, striking fear deeper into Kele's heart.

She entered the room as the guard hobbled in and collapsed on his palette. Uneke shook the figure of the other guard, curled up on his own palette, and jolted back.

"Is he sick, too?" Kele asked, her voice a whisper.

Uneke pursed her lips, then opened them, but her lips merely trembled.

"Uneke?" Kele tried again, but Uneke said nothing.

Kele walked to the sleeping guard, and put her hand on his head. At first, she was surprised. It was not hot at all, and then it struck her—it was cold. Far, far too cold.

Kele let out a small shriek, and she rushed back to Uneke, grasping her arm.

"What do we do?" Uneke asked.

Kele didn't know. She didn't know at all.

—

Kele didn't know how long she stood in the guards' room, clutching Uneke's arm, the two of them motionless, petrified. It could have been seconds, minutes, or even hours.

After that unknown interval, Kele found thoughts of her training surfacing in her mind. She let go of Uneke, moved to the side of the dead guard, and began saying prayers for him. When she'd finished, she found Uneke standing over the other guard, who lay twitching on his palette.

Uneke looked at Kele with the most distraught expression on her face, her lips poised to speak, but unable to release the words. At any rate, the utterance was clear—this guard's condition was deteriorating by the minute.

A thought pierced Kele's mind, and she did speak it: "Alíza!"

Uneke's eyes shot open wide, and the two of them rushed together out the door, down the hall and back to their room, the beams of the ship creaking as they jostled against the impact of the waves.

Back in their room, they found Alíza shivering as though she were cold, and her teeth chattering, although she was still warm to the touch and dripping sweat, now pooling on her palette.

"We will pray for her—" Kele started.

"Isn't there something we should get? Some herb? A doctor amongst the crew, maybe?"

"In order to do that, we would have to leave her alone. Again. We should stay together. It's the only defense we have." Kele knelt down beside Alíza, set her forearms together before her, and closed her eyes.

When she'd finished praying, she opened her eyes to find Uneke was praying as well. She waited patiently for her sister to finish. When Uneke did finish, her eyes fluttered open and she let her arms collapse in front of her. She said nothing, merely gazed at the floor. She looked utterly haggard, emotionally spent.

Kele, on the other hand, felt oddly lucid. Fear was present, sure, but in this moment, she found that, rather than paralyzing her, it was the raw fuel propelling her thoughts.

"Food and water," Kele said.

Uneke turned her head and at stared at her blankly.

"The sun will be up soon," Kele said. "We need to figure out how to get ourselves food and water, as the people who used to do that for us are... unable to now. Depending on how much is available, we might also wash Alíza, though I have no idea if that would help or harm her at this point."

Uneke's gaze drifted toward the floor of their cabin.

A moan punctured the silence, emanating from somewhere in the ship.

"I'll go," Kele said.

Uneke's head jerked up and her gaze contacted Kele's again.

"I'll search the ship for water, food, and other supplies," Kele said.

"You can't go alone."

"And if we both go, Alíza will be left alone."

Uneke shook her head, but couldn't seem to muster a verbal argument to that one. "Wait for sun up," she muttered.

Kele nodded.

She and Uneke sat at Alíza's bedside, saying prayers every so often, and watching out the porthole for the glow on the horizon that would displace the aquamarine light of the moons.

When the sun did finally peak above the horizon, Kele stood and left her cabin, while Uneke remained seated and praying.

The first thing Kele did was check on the sick guard, who she discovered was now also dead. She said a prayer for him and hurried out of that cabin of death.

She crept down the hall, then climbed up the familiar ladder to the deck. At the top, she let her head just peak over the porthole, and she scanned the entire deck—deserted.

Kele clambered up off the ladder and stood on the deck, surveying her surroundings. No land in sight in any direction. The sky was clear. It would be a good day. At least the gods had granted them fair weather to accompany the horror of plague.

Having exhausted the parts of the ship she knew well, she decided to begin her search with what lay beyond the porthole on the other side of the deck, the one the crew were always using, but which she and the other priestesses had been instructed to avoid.

She took a deep breath and marched toward it.

As she approached, a pained moan erupted, much louder than any she had previously heard, and it seemed to have emanated from somewhere below the dark porthole she now stood before.

Fear paralyzed her in that moment, held her fast, and her muscles tensed up completely. Then she remembered Uneke and Alíza, and her muscles relaxed, her mind cleared. She grasped the ladder in the porthole and descended.

At the bottom, she found a hallway much like the one that led to the priestesses' cabin. She began walking down it, very slowly, listening carefully, but the only noises she heard were the sounds of the sea, the water sloshing against the ship, and the boards creaking in response.

A room appeared on her right, this hallway apparently being a mirror layout to hers, in which the rooms were on the left. She peered inside and found nothing but the corpses of seamen. She hurried on down to the next, which presented two corpses and two very ill seaman, rolling on their palettes.

She began running, passing four then five rooms of

the sick and the dead. She began to feel lightheaded, and wondered if that was the result of witnessing so much death, of being enshrouded in pestilence, or perhaps she was becoming ill herself.

She stopped at the fifth doorway, knelt, and said a prayer for all those she had seen, then a short one for Uneke and Alíza, before hurrying onward.

At the end of the hallway, she found another porthole and another ladder, one which must have led into the very bowels of the ship. Peering in, it looked pitch black in that bottom level. That made sense. There would be no windows there, otherwise water would rush in and the ship would sink.

She took a deep breath. Her eyes would adjust with time. And it would make sense to store the food and water there. She remembered Uneke and Alíza. Alíza, whose life might still be perhaps saved, with Isórrop's guidance. Quelling her nerves anew, Kele descended into the darkness.

When she reached the bottom of the ladder, she turned slowly around and scanned the inky landscape. She could make out nothing at first, only vague lines, ones she wasn't even sure were there, but slowly, her eyes adjusted, and the outlines of boxes and barrels emerged from the void.

She spotted a barrel near her that had been left open. She put her head close and sniffed—dried meat. She pulled the lid off another nearby barrel and discovered fruit. She allowed herself a moment's feeling of victory, and found it appropriately punctured by a moan from somewhere above her, a struck a chord of fear within her anew.

She replaced the lid of the barrel and began pulling open others. She wound her way around the heaps of supplies, moving away from food and into area of ropes, giant iron pins, extra sails, and other seafaring equipment. She then moved into a section of textiles, ceramics, and other goods. Amongst those she found those chests that the diplomats had planned to present to Akhtm. She realized she hadn't seen either them or the generals since the outbreak, and she said a quick prayer for their health and safety.

At the far end of the hold, she opened a barrel and discovered—she smelled it just to make sure—yes, it was water. Wooden cups were stacked on a shelf against the wall to her left. She filled one cup, then took it with her back to the part of the hold with the food. Realizing she would need at least one hand to climb the ladders, she tore off the top half of her robe—praying Isórrop's forgiveness—and folded it into an impromptu sack, which she loaded up with fruit and meat. The rest of her robe she wrapped around her waist.

Now she only had to make it back to her cabin.

She returned to the ladder, where she took the cup and the sack in one hand and climbed with the other. A wave jostled the ship, and she nearly spilled the water, but after that near miss, she proceeded more carefully, until she reached the porthole into hallway, where she was able to set down her things on the floor and pull the rest of herself up.

Kele righted herself, stood, and was nearly ready to lean down and pick up her things, when a sight caught her eye and held her fast. At the end of the hallway stood a man, his features shrouded in the relative darkness of the hallway. He appeared a cloudy outline of a person, all the light coming from the porthole and the rooms behind him. His hands seemed unnaturally elongated until Kele realized that there was actually a rope dangling from each of his hands, not held, but fastened at his wrists—bonds, which had been severed.

Instinctively, Kele pulled up her torn robes to cover as much of her chest as she could. The man in the hall remained motionless. She couldn't even tell if he was facing toward her or behind her.

She opened her mouth to call out to him, but no sound emerged.

She remembered the break-in, the way her voice simply caught in her throat, fear stifling her voice. She steadied her breathing, prayed to the god for strength, and tried again.

"Hello?" Her voice worked that time.

The man started making noises Kele couldn't identify. His shoulders were collapsing, shuddering, and, was he crying?

"I'm Kele, priestess of the cult of Isórrop," she called out.

The man's voice came out a raspy whisper, which Kele could only barely make out from down the hall. "It's my time, then?"

"Your time?" Kele called out. "I don't understand."

The man began marching toward her, and fear rose up within Kele, boiling over.

"I don't—" Her voice caught, but she righted her thoughts and recalled her training. "I don't want to hurt you. Do not come any nearer!"

He continued marching. "Leave me alone," he roared. "Tell them all to leave me alone!"

She felt the urge to back up, but she had been trained not to pin her back to a wall. She forced herself to take up her defensive stance instead. The man's features hove into view. A dark, scraggly mop of hair and sad, sunken, red, deranged eyes appeared beneath a shot of sunlight bursting through the door of a chamber of sick seamen. And then he was past it, again a shadowy spectre lumbering toward her.

"I'm sorry already!" He took a swipe at her, which she ducked to avoid, then sidestepped around him. "Why can't you just leave me alone?!" He lunged at her legs, and she jumped, easily landing on his exposed back and toppling him.

"Stop this at once!" She found herself surprisingly confident, her foot on the small of his back. "I am a *priestess* of the *cult* of *Isórrop*. Whoever you fear, it is not me."

He sobbed into the floor, then reeled up all at once, toppling her. That had been stupid mistake. But she rolled away, righted herself on one foot, looked up, and nearly avoided a collision as the man barreled toward her. She threw herself back and to the side, then pushed him past herself.

She righted herself into a proper defensive stance, and only then became aware of the fact that she was angry with this man. She wanted to get back to Alíza and Uneke, and this horrible man was in the way, but she was forgetting that Isórrop had compassion for all people, this man included, and as Isórrop's disciple, she'd been trained to share that compassion, even in times such as these.

"Someone has hurt you," Kele called out to him as he scrambled to his feet and turned. "Who hurt you? Who do you think I am?"

"I don't want to die."

"I am *not* going to hurt you. There's a plague on this ship. My friends are in trouble. I need to get them food and water. Please let me pass."

He remained motionless, his chest rising and falling while his eyes streamed tears.

"My name is Kele," she tried again. "I am a priestess of the cult of Isórrop. I am at your service, if you will only tell me…"

"Furies." A cold, stark utterance, loud but flat.

"Furies?" It had been some time since she had heard the word, but she remembered the tales—demons of Ahdez that witches were supposedly able to conjure up to Earth. In the tales, the witches invariably chose some victim, and furies would torment him (always a "him") and drive him insane. But furies were not part of any pantheon or official cult. As a priestess of Isórrop, the very topic was beneath her.

He looked at her, his face seeming to move through pain, then to anger in her silence.

"Furies," she said again, this time matter-of-factly. "I doubt any furies would dare come near a priestess of Isórrop, so we had better stop this fighting and stick together, shall we?"

The man looked at the floor momentarily. "Torsen," he mumbled. "My name was Torsen. But no one calls me that anymore."

"What do they call you?" Kele asked.

Torsen was silent for many moments. "Murderer." Then, softer. "Kin-murderer."

Kele gulped. That explained Alíza's odd request. Priestesses sharing a ship with such a man? It occurred to her that she might lose her priesthood for even speaking with him. Though, as long as Uneke and Alíza were in trouble, she would do whatever it took to keep them safe, from Torsen, from illness, from the elements, or anything else.

Kele decided it was time to stop looming over him, and to sit. She set herself crosslegged on the deck, another moan rising up from somewhere on the ship. She adopted her most calming voice. "May I call you Torsen?"

He nodded, then sniffled. At least he didn't seem angry anymore.

"Why are you going to Akhtm?"

"Trial."

"I didn't think... such trials... needed another city's legal council—?"

"This one does."

Kele shook her head. "What city are you from?"

"Stheno."

That was a large and powerful mainland city. "Why does Stheno need Ahktm for—?"

"Because she killed my father. Then I killed her."

Kele's eyes widened. It was a wonder that his hallucinations were limited to furies. That he was able to have a conversation at all was astounding.

"I saw you, when you boarded the ship. There were others with you. Are they—?"

"When I woke up, my best friend, Dylápe, was already dead. Three guards were sick, another dead. I thought the furies took them to punish me."

"Were you asleep a very long time?"

He nodded vigorously. "They made me chew some root, whenever I woke up. It made me feel relaxed, but also distant from my body, and tired. I slept a lot. But then I woke up, and everyone was sick. So I found a hook on the deck and used it to saw through my bonds..."

Torsen continued his story, but Kele's mind had fixated on the details on of Torsen incarceration, her eyes went wide with realization. A whole ship full of people, a plague which terminated its victims inside twenty-four hours, and two people had remained mysteriously unaffected, both of whom—

She stood up. "Torsen," she commanded. "I need to go back to my chamber. My friends need my help. Are you able to help?"

He stared at the floor, his dark hair concealing his eyes.

"Torsen!"

"Yes," he said. "I'll go with you."

Back in her cabin, she found Alíza in convulsions, probably the final stage of the illness, and Uneke lying on her palette shivering and moaning. Kele went straight to their chest of possessions, threw open the lid, and began sifting through the contents, throwing things on the floor to get them out of her way.

"Aha!" she announced finding the sack of root.

She broke off a piece of it, and put it into Uneke's hand. "Chew," Kele commanded.

She then moved to Alíza's side. "Alíza? Alíza! Can you hear me? Alíza?" It was no good. Her elder sister's eyes were rolling back in her head, and she was spasming out of all control. If Kele put the root in her mouth, it would probably choke her.

She turned to Torsen, who'd been standing just outside the door, a modest gesture of attempting to keep his distance from priestesses. "She can't chew. But if I chop up the root finely enough, maybe I can get her to drink it. I need a knife and a cup of water."

"I can do this for you, but if they drink and eat from utensils I touch—"

"I will ask Isórrop's forgiveness when Alíza is beyond danger." She looked at her sisters, still shivering and convulsing respectively, then moved closer to the doorway. "It will be our secret. Go."

Torsen nodded and dashed down the hallway.

Kele tended to her sisters while she waited. She worried that Torsen would fall victim to his madness on the way, or perhaps he would use the opportunity to gather weapons of some kind. She preferred to think that she'd established a kind of meager connection with him. One person, who was willing to engage with him, despite his offense, and despite her station.

Before many minutes had passed, she heard clambering in the hallway, and Torsen appeared at the door, indeed carrying a cup of water, and a small bag, which contained a knife and a cutting board. Torsen set them just inside the door, and backed into the hall.

"Thank you." Kele smiled at him as she gathered

them up.

She quickly diced the root as small as she could make it, put the bits into the water, and stirred with the end of the knife. The hardest part was getting Alíza to drink, and she spilled much of it on herself, but she managed to get some of it down.

Kele set the cup at the door. "More water, please."

Torsen ran off.

Kele moved to Uneke's side. "How are you feeling?"

"Better, I think..." Uneke mumbled.

Kele felt her forehead, which wasn't as warm as when she'd arrived.

"Who was that at the door?"

"Just a kind soul," Kele said. "Someone willing to help."

When Alíza stopped convulsing, Kele announced to Uneke that she would be doing rounds of the rest of the ship. Saving themselves would be pointless if all the sailors died and no one was left to operate the ship.

Kele left her sister with a small amount of the root, just in case either of their symptoms returned, and took the rest with her. She took Torsen, who was standing just outside the door, like a guard, and together the two of them scoured the ship for those still struggling against the plague.

While Torsen had demonstrated great reservation going anywhere near Kele's sisters, he had no qualms ministering to others aboard the ship. He distributed the root, instructed them to chew, and held them down if they were convulsing, while Kele poured root-water down their throats.

The ship's captain and second-in-command were both dead, but Kele and Torsen were able to save five sailors, two Fidian diplomats, one Fidian general, and one of the Sthenian soldiers assigned to guard Torsen. By the time they had reached everyone who could be saved, only the stub of the root remained.

In the hallway outside the diplomats' cabin, Kele let out a deep breath. She gave Torsen a small smile.

Torsen returned a weak smile. "I should... go back to my cabin. They will be better soon, and..."

He didn't finish the sentence, but she fully understood. It would not be wise for them to be seen moving about together for much longer.

Kele nodded.

"I'm sorry," he said very suddenly. "When I thought— earlier, I thought— I'm sorry I attacked you."

"I forgive you, Torsen."

A wave of calm seemed to descend on him in that moment. In his eyes, just for a moment, Kele sensed warmth and ease—even balance. For just a moment. Clouds of concern returned almost immediately.

"I'll get going, then," he said.

"Good luck," Kele said. And she proceeded in the opposite direction down the hall, back toward her own cabin.

When she had returned, Uneke was crouched over Alíza.

"Is she still improving?" Kele asked.

Uneke stood, nodded and walked toward her.

"How did you know?" she asked with a wry smile. "About the root?"

Kele cracked a smile of her own. "By the will and grace of Isórrop, through whom all things are possible." Including, Kele realized, learning how to be afraid.

SOMETHING NOVEL

a wave peaks
gulls cackle and squirm about the sky
they plummet to the sea, one by one
the shore is clear
but the sky
blood red and dangerous
the birds fill their beaks with fish
and the fisherman stare at the shore
their bellies empty
yet their stores full
lights blink on in the city
for tonight—

The journeyman proctor in the front row shot to his feet, an event which registered too late in Kháll's peripheral vision. "Thank you!" the proctor called out nervously.

Kháll clenched the scroll tightly and glared at the proctor, who strode toward the podium and entered Kháll's personal space, forcing him away from the podium. Kháll narrowed his eyes and his heard the sound of his own heart pounding in his eardrums. He was probably perspiring, too. He opened his mouth to speak, but the proctor beat him to it. "You're out of time."

Like hell, Kháll thought as he marched back to his seat, crushing his poem in his grip. *You let the first guy go on for ten fucking minutes.*

The proctor began introducing the next applicant, but the sound of his voice was mettrs away. Kháll threw himself into his seat, and only briefly caught Mitri's glance. Those big, beautiful brown eyes always calmed him, but the sound of the proctor's voice grated, and Kháll found his attention drifting back toward the stage.

"Stay," Mitri whispered in Kháll's ear.

"Why the hell should I?" He'd intended it a whisper, but it came out louder.

Mitri's voice became firmer. "It will look bad for you to leave. Don't you want to read next time?"

No, Kháll thought. He focused on breathing in through his nose and out through thinly pursed lips. Mitri had told him to do that when he needed to calm down, but this time it didn't seem to be helping.

"We're really excited to hear this next young poet," the proctor announced to the entire crowd of thirty assembled poets, both guildbound and aspiring. "He comes to us from the township of Ezos near Sóf. I first heard him read at the Assembly Hall last Autumn. I think you're all in for a treat. Please welcome Pragog Chyló."

"Listen to him," Mitri whispered into Kháll's ear, enunciating each syllable meticulously. "Learn what you can from him, and incorporate it into your work."

Only for you, Mitri. I will do this, but only for you.

Kháll found his breaths steadying and his heart rate slowing down. He took a long, deep breath in and out as silently as he could. He would listen and learn. If the guild loved this Chyló guy so much, perhaps he could learn something.

Pragog Chyló stood up from a seat in the second row from the front. His hair was bushy and unkempt, and he had a round, pocked face. Probably some wealthy farmer's son. Some of them got into sports, but the ones who didn't tended to get fat on meat and cream. This guy looked like he hadn't done an ounce of hard labor in his life.

Kháll bristled and felt his grasp on solemnity slipping away as Pragog waddled up to the podium.

"Thank you, proctor," Pragog said with a smarmy smile. "The poem I wish to read tonight is titled 'My Dearest Flatulence.'"

A laugh resounded from the crowd and Kháll's face flushed red. Far from laughing, he bit his tongue. Mitri cast a very long, sideways gaze Kháll's way, but Kháll didn't care in the least. He let his breaths grow longer and deeper, struggling to keep his affectations invisible.

Pragog stood tall and adopted his authorial speaking voice.

> *My dearest flatulence,*
> *Why do you always visit me*
> *at the most inopportune of times?*
> *The dinner table is no place for*
> *your foul odor.*

The crowd erupted in stitches of laughter.

> *And certainly, when I finally*
> *ask the beautiful girl from lyceum*
> *to go out on my yacht,*
> *your uproarious belching*
> *from my rear*
> *prevents me from scoring*
> *so much needed recreation.*

More laughter from the crowd.

Pragog continued, but his words had drifted to edge of Kháll's perceptions. Indignity and rage flooded Kháll's vision red, and if he had held a javelin, knife, or hell, he'd take a discus or a rock, he'd have hurled it at the nearest target—the fat moron, the proctor, or any of the idiot crowd would do—or perhaps he would have a nice little homicidal rampage.

Kháll lurched from his seat, just as the crowd erupted in another flurry of laughter. Pragog had begun making fart noises with his mouth. Kháll felt Mitri's hand on his arm, but threw it away and stormed away to the back of the auditorium and out into the cool air of Sóf's evening streets. The cold felt good against his overheating face and arms, but inside he burned with more fiery rage, and he possessed fuel in spades.

"Kháll!" Mitri grabbed his arm again, but Kháll threw him off and continued marching down the street.

"I don't want to hear it."

"Tough, you're going to have to."

"This is bullshit, Mitri!"

Passersby shot him glances, and someone whispered something about dockworkers being callous, unruly, and crude in the city, but Kháll could not summon any energy with which to care.

"You're making a scene," Mitri observed.

"Damn right I am! Flatulence? Seriously? If the guild would rather apprentice a fat clown to perform stupid fart jokes instead of a philosopher interested in exploring themes topical for humanity, then what the fuck is the point?"

"The point is I'm not letting you give up." Mitri

grasped Kháll's arm tight and didn't let go, despite Kháll's thrashing.

"Damn it, Mitri! Let go!"

"No. You're going to go back there tomorrow and you're going to audition again. You're going home and you're going to write a new poem."

"What about? The ethical implications of my butt crack? Fuck that."

"No." Mitri huffed. "You don't have to write something stupid. But you do have to write something that will get their attention."

"I don't want their attention!" Kháll roared and threw away Mitri's grasp with a violent thrash of his arm. "They're clearly too fucking stupid to waste any more of my precious time on!"

Kháll marched away down the street. He slammed his feet into the ground with each step, thinking about how much he hated the entire Poets' Guild. All the masters, all the lorecrafters, all the journeymen, all the apprentices, and especially Pragog Chyló, who would certainly have an apprenticeship within the week. For his fart joke poem.

Fuck them all.

He turned left, pounded across another block, then turned right.

His house sat at the end of the street, a modest but solid brick construction. Candlelight glowed from the windows.

Kháll marched in the door, and Mitri stormed in alongside him. Typical.

Mom and dad were nowhere in sight, but his sisters' voices were a gentle murmur from the kitchen. His parents were probably still taking care of the shop they ran in the market district, the one that paid for all of this. Kháll supposed he would have to go help them now. He'd have to learn math and use his scroll paper for tabulating money.

The thought made him nauseous.

His nausea turned to hatred—hatred for his scrolls.

He marched up the staircase, and the sound of Mitri's footsteps followed him.

"Kháll?"

"What?"

"What are you doing?"

Kháll bunched of his lips. He threw open the door to his room, ran to his desk, grabbed up whatever poems he'd left there. He found them only by muscle memory, the entire space being shrouded in darkness. He grabbed up the papers and he pulled as hard as he could. The sickening, shredding tear filled the entire room.

"Kháll!" Mitri's silhouette roared from the doorway.

Kháll tore a second, then a third time, and each time his anger intensified. He threw the tatters to the floor, grabbed at the edge of his desk, and pulled until the whole thing flipped and crashed to the floor. His remaining poems and blank scrolls and ink wells and pens tumbled and spilled, splattering black blotches as they went.

Mitri turned Kháll around, grabbed Kháll's chin and pressed Kháll's lips onto his own. Kháll's fiery rage took a hairpin turn. He seized Mitri's chest, pulled their bodies together, and returned the kiss passionately. In a froth of testosterone, he tore at Mitri's robe until it lay in a heap on the floor, then he rushed to shut the door to his room and threw off his own robe.

They rolled onto Kháll's bed amidst the ink stains. Mitri pushed a few stray pens to the floor.

An hour later, Kháll found his anger emptied and his fuel stores, of all kinds, spent.

Kháll watched as Mitri climbed out of Kháll's bed. He liked Mitri's back muscles most of all, his broad shoulders, too. Mitri grabbed up his loincloth and wrapped it around his waist and between his legs, and then pulled on his light-green robes, covering up his beautiful upper back.

Mitri carved the male form well. Two years ago, he'd gotten his hands on a large hunk of granite, which had turned out to have too many impurities for a construction worker and mutual friend. The friend had sold it to Mitri at a discount, and Mitri had promptly lost himself to carving for three months straight. The stone had gone from an amorphous, unevenly cut blob to a bare-chested man with curly hair holding a scroll—Mitri's rendering of Sofáan, the God of Wisdom.

"He's the god of wisdom, not fertility," Khàll had quietly joked when the outline of the figure had become clear. Mitri had carved it in the grove behind his home, a place the two of them had often gone to fool around, since Mitri's nearest neighbors were over a thousand mettrs distant.

That statue, however, had landed Mitri an apprenticeship in the Sculptor's Guild. Assuming he didn't break any bylaws, he was set for life. Khàll didn't begrudge him the acceptance, but it did make his own inability to convince the Poets' Guild of his worth all that much harder to bear.

Mitri sat now, gazing at the floor, but it had grown utterly dark, and the only light was the faint glow of Stathro from the window. Khàll pulled himself up in bed to get a better view of what Mitri was doing. He thought to reach out for the lantern, then realized that he'd overturned his desk and that must now be somewhere in the mess on the floor, and probably broken, too.

"What's up?" Khàll asked.

"I'm not sure." Mitri rapped his fist against the floorboards. "You got another lantern?"

Khàll pulled himself out of bed and scrambled to find his own loincloth and robes. "Just a sec."

Mitri continued rapping his fist against the floor near Khàll's overturned desk. He pulled on his robes and fetched the smaller, crummier lantern he kept in his closet. He righted a stool near the desk, set the lantern atop it, lit it, and held it over Mitri's head.

A dull orange glow bathed Mitri's hand as he wrapped again, first one floorboard, then another, the second one sounding hollow. The second floorboard jittered and wobbled as Mitri knocked at it.

"Is it even fixed?" Khváll asked.

Mitri shrugged. "You tell me. It's your floor."

Khváll grabbed at the floorboard's edges and pulled. It came off easily. Khváll set it to the side, and Mitri grabbed the lantern and held it over the hole. The small space looked much like one would expect—globs of dried clay and flecks of wood—but there also lay a small, green box with gilded edges, that just peaked out and glinted from beneath a thick layer of dust.

Khváll and Mitri cast each other glances.

"Is that yours?" Mitri asked.

Khváll shook his head.

"Who had this room before you?"

Khváll pulled the box carefully up out of the floor. "No one."

"None of your sisters?"

"No. It's been my room since we moved here."

Khváll blew at the dust layer atop the box, sending a cloud of the stuff flying across the remnants of his desk. He pulled the lid slowly open. Scrolls appeared within, a row of seven of them, the parchment yellowed and withered. Each was tied with a tiny red ribbon.

"Who lived here before you?" Mitri asked.

"Not sure. My parents bought it from someone, but I don't know who"

Kháll set the box down, and carefully pulled up the scroll closest to the front of the box. To his surprise, another row of scrolls was layered below the first. Briefly appraising the box, Kháll guessed that it held a third layer, too.

He carefully untied the ribbon and pulled the scroll open. Kháll held it out against the candlelight, and both of them gazed over the words. It was written using the standard Palípolian alphabet, but the dialect was distinctly Sófan. The handwriting was neat and legible. Kháll recognized ligatures too, the ones that Ignu taught in his introduction to poetics. Whoever had written this had been prepped for the Poets' Guild.

"Is Perip a god you've heard of?" Mitri asked.

Kháll tilted his head, confused, and Mitri nodded at the words. Kháll took to actually reading the words, an within a few lines realized that Perip was the topic of the poem, presumably some god. Kháll frowned. "Never heard of him."

Mitri furrowed his brow and huffed. "Is this even poetry?"

Kháll could only shake his head. The text moved in one stream of letters, without line breaks to delimit stanzas, and the meter was unlike anything he'd ever seen. It was almost as if the author had been oblivious to meter. Or hadn't cared about it. "I'm not sure," Kháll replied.

Mitri widened his eyes and shook his head. "You're not pulling my leg, are you?"

Kháll shook his head, though confused as he was, his found the text drawing him further and further into its grasp. Which was so odd, because the words were utterly unpoetic. The text spoke of an unknown god—perhaps not even a god, just some human. Was this Perip the author? It couldn't be the author, could it? Already on the first scroll he was winning tournaments and marrying the most beautiful woman of his city, which was named Teleio, not a city Kháll had ever heard of. Yet, the text also spoke of Teleio being in Palípoli. How could that be? Unless Kháll's geography teacher had been an imbecile, which seemed hardly possible for Sóf.

The meter was jagged and uneven, and yet the text was utterly immersive.

"It's beautiful," Kháll muttered.

Mitri glanced a few times between Kháll the scroll he held. "Really?"

"Yes."

"I thought you said the meter's wrong."

"It's... This isn't how meter is supposed to be done. I mean, it's not how they teach us to do it. But this is still beautiful. I think so, anyway."

Mitri bunched up his face. "You ready for the next scroll yet?"

"Just a sec." Kháll had in fact finished, but he was still re-reading lines, trying to feel for meter in his mind, find that something that was responsible for the harmony amongst the discord.

Eventually, he wrapped the first scroll carefully up, and snatched up the second.

He and Mitri sat reading scrolls by candlelight for hours, immersing themselves in the world of of Perip and his imaginary city of Teleio. Perip journeyed out to sea, beyond the Palípolian islands and discovered new islands filled with impossible creatures, each of whom he thwarted and tamed. Just as Perip had arrived at his third new island, two sets of footsteps emanated from the hall-way outside Kháll's room.

Mitri stood and tiptoed toward the window, avoiding stepping on the strewn desk remnants. "Stathro isn't even visible anymore," Mitri whispered. "Probably only a couple of hours to sunrise."

"Stay here," Kháll whispered back.

Mitri pursed his lips. He wouldn't say it, but they both knew it. They were approaching the age when they were supposed to get married. No one cared about teenagers who fooled around with one another, so long as they went out and got respectable jobs and got respectably married once they finished their studies. Carrying on at twenty-one would be perceived as childish.

All Kháll knew was that he wanted to spend more time with Mitri. The whole thing about marriage was annoying and inconvenient, and the idea of sex with a woman held no appeal whatsoever. There were plenty of unmarried men in both their guilds, but none who spent quite so much time together as he and Mitri did, or if they did, they did it much more discreetly than Kháll and Mitri.

Mitri broke a wan smile. "All right."

Kháll put the scroll back into its box, put the box back beneath the floor, and replaced the loose floorboard.

The two of them disrobed again and climbed into Kháll's bed.

"Tomorrow night," Mitri said, "we're going to clean up the mess you made."

"Okay, mom."

Kháll felt a playful elbow jab to his side, and he giggled.

Kháll first stirred when the weight on his bed shifted, and he woke up properly when the latch to his bedroom door clicked shut. He felt for Mitri, but finding nothing but pillow, he craned his neck upward to look about the room.

The disaster he had made of his bedside the prior evening now dominated the scene. He'd nicked up the legs of the desk in overturning it. Huge blots of ink dotted the floor, including two huge, goopy stains where his two ink wells lay on their sides. Only the stool with its snuffed lantern atop it sat orderly amongst the chaos.

Had the box been real? Perhaps he'd imagined it.

Kháll scrambled out of bed, and found the floorboard still unnailed. He pried it off and the box lay within. Daring a glance out his window, he gauged that he had no more than an hour before he'd be expected at the press. They'd probably send him out harvesting reeds today anyway. Still, he snatched up the box, opened it, and found the scroll where he'd stopped the night before.

Just one scroll, he told himself, but he read three before he finally sealed the scrolls and the box away, threw on his robes, and ran out the door without a word to his family.

He knew he was in trouble by the foot traffic on the roads—it was thin, meaning that most people were already at work. He quickened his pace, but by the time he'd passed through the Sóf city gates, followed the main road into the furnace district, and then finally pulled open the huge metal door to pressworks, he found all his coworkers already manning the enormous stations where they ground, laid, rolled, and heated endik reeds into scroll paper.

"Get to pulling," the pressmaster called from the vats, with only a glance, and not a pleased one.

With a sigh, Kháll turned and strode back out the door. He grabbed up one of the wicker baskets from the alley, then made his way downhill, away from the furnace district, out of the north gates and to the riverbank, where, alongside his coworkers, he pulled at the sticky and prickly endik reeds at the banks of the river.

He filled only two baskets before lunch and three after. His mind kept straying back to the scrolls hidden within his room.

First, there was the question of what kind of writing they represented. The rules of poetics were clear: poetry was metered; it was for the exploration of human concerns and those of the gods. Those of the gods had to be expounded with the help of a temple initiate or higher. A writer wasn't allowed to craft those alone.

Now the Bards' Guild did tell unmetered stories about the gods without considering the temples' wishes as closely, but they never wrote them down, so the high priests considered this less of a threat to their authority.

What was he to do with an unmetered story about human concerns that didn't seem to be a biography of any sort. Its characters and events were invented—at least partially, unless there actually was a city of Teleio no one had ever heard of. But what seemed more likely was that the author had simply invented the city and the protagonist from his imagination. And although Perip seemed physically and mentally stalwart, he was decidedly not a god.

An entirely novel narrative form had sat beneath the floorboards of his room for how long? He'd worked at the press long enough to know that paper had a life about three times that of a human. There were jobs in the Poets' Guild for those who would do nothing but copy—the job that Kháll worried he'd end up in if he didn't get accepted as a poet soon. That or he could continue pulling and pressing reeds for the rest of his life.

The writer of the scrolls in his room had to have been a member of the last family who had lived there, or perhaps the family before them, but probably not beyond that.

Khállll tugged and tugged at the prickly reeds. His hands had grown calloused long ago, and now he felt only a dull scratching. Finally, as he filled his third basket of the afternoon, the sun had drawn low enough in the sky, and his coworkers began to disappear from the riverside.

He dumped his final basketful of reeds into the collection bin in the alley behind the pressworks building, threw down the basket itself in the heap beside the bin, and ran off into the city proper.

The streets were busy, but he ignored the people around him. They were obstacles to be dodged. Singlemindedly, he made his way to his parents' shop, pulled open the wooden door, and walked inside.

The apothecary always smelled of something different. His parents did that to hide the smells of the chemicals. Today it was cinnamon aroma that wafted about, mixed with something he couldn't identify… maybe an alcohol. Bottles lined the walls containing tinctures of varying colors, though most were clear.

His father stood in front of the counter, talking to an elderly women. She prattled on and on about her grandchildren, and Khálll found himself annoyed on two fronts—she was keeping him away from talking to his father, and she was filling his father's mind with tales of grandchildren. He wished one of his sisters would hurry up and get old enough to get married.

Finally, the woman turned and cast Khall a disapproving glance before hobbling out of the store.

"Hi, dad."

His father scooped up some coins, dropped them in a box, then began scrawling on a piece of parchment. "Evening, Khall. Did you bring that paper I asked for?"

Khall winced. He'd intended to pick it up after the poetry reading auditions the night before. And he'd just come from work, so he really had no excuse. "I'm really sorry. The reading went badly. I should have gotten them this morning. I can run down there and pick up some now—"

"Do that." His father was frowning and still writing, though he should have been able to complete the tabulation of a simple transaction by now.

"I need to know though…" Khall paused momentarily. His father had that look in his eyes that meant his patience was being tried. "Just, dad. One question. Then I'll go pick the paper up and come right back. Who lived in our house before us?"

His father looked up, now more inquisitive than anything else. "Why?"

"Just curious." He carefully controlled all his actions. He held eye contact. He held his hands behind his back. His father was shrewd, but so was Kháll. That mercantile streak in his family would be good something, at least.

"A married couple," his father said. "No children. I can't remember their name. It was a long time ago."

"Is there a record anywhere?"

"Not at home, but the council keeps certified deeds going back at least a century. What's this all about?"

"Nothing. I'll go get that paper now. Really sorry." He turned to run out of the shop.

"Kháll?" His father's voice sounded more hurt than upset.

He turned back to face his father. "Yeah, dad?"

"Your mother and I are worried about you. We'd like you to start focusing on an apprenticeship." All his facial muscles tensed. "Maybe it's time to let go of certain friends who might be holding you back."

Kháll started to answer, but stopped. He'd started to say that he loved Mitri and he'd never betray him, not even for family, but he couldn't say that. It would be disastrous.

Thankfully, before either of them could say anything, the door open and a middle-aged man walked into the shop.

"Hello," his father said jovially to the patron.

Kháll hurried out the door before the man could close it behind himself.

—

213

Kháll ran down the country road as fast as his feet could take him. The dirt path wound between the rounded mounds of hills covered in green grasses and fence-delineated fields and spotted with trees. The Early Summer sun blazed and sweat dripped down his back despite the evening breeze. He clutched the green box under his right arm.

The familiar country house came into view. Mitri stood in the front yard, hacking into an enormous upright log with a knife. He turned and smiled as Kháll approached.

Kháll held out the box. "I finished it."

"And?"

"It's incredible. You should read it."

Mitri nodded, pocketed his knife and nodded toward the path that led around the house. This was a usual routine. The work shed in Mitri's back yard was guaranteed to offer them privacy, Mitri's parents and brothers always off in one field or another.

They rounded the house and continued down the hill into a wooded grove that followed a stream running between the hills. Mitri opened the door to his work shed, and they ducked inside. Kháll had only just closed the door when Mitri wrapped his arms around him and kissed him passionately. With a start, Kháll remembered they hadn't seen each other now for two days, but he hadn't realized how much time had passed since he'd been so absorbed in figuring out who the story belonged to.

"Mitri..." Kháll said between kisses. "Mitri, listen."

"Yeah?" Mitri asked, still running his hands up and down Kháll's torso. "My dad mentioned... people are starting to notice..."

"I don't care." Mitri kissed him again. "Not now."

Kháll's own suppressed lust surged forth, and he submitted to it. He stashed the green box atop the nearby worktable, and both of them fell onto the cot and removed one another's robes.

Some time afterward, with Mitri wrapped in his arms, he whispered, "I found out who the author was."

"Oh?" Mitri shuffled around so they could see one another's eyes.

"His name was Synai Tymó. He lived in my house until he was twenty-five. He moved to Meigá for work and his parents sold the house to my parents."

"Did you find the parents, at least?"

"No. They apparently moved out into the country. Could be anywhere between here and Apmonómen."

"How do you know that Tymó went to Meigá then?"

Kháll chortled. "I looked him up in the Poets' Guild registry."

"Was he a member?"

"He was banned from attending both reading auditions and general performances."

Mitri furrowed his brow. "And so he moved to Meigá?"

"Yeah. To become a stage performer."

"Huh."

"I want to go look for him."

Mitri scrunched his brow harder. "Why?"

"Because he created something amazing. Mitri, these scrolls... this is something completely and totally new. So many poets are just rehashing the same stories about the gods that the bards have been telling for decades, or telling 'new' stories with the same structures and archetypes that have existed for just as long. Tymó did what I want to do—he created something totally unique and still beautiful. I need to find out why he didn't go to the guild with this. Why he just shoved it in a box and stuck it under the floorboards in his house."

Mitri looked at him silently a long time. "What will the pressmaster say?"

Kháll shook his head. "I don't care. Mitri... I want you to come with me."

Mitri's vague unease morphed to shocked distress. "But the Sculptor's Guild... my apprenticeship..."

"I can see the way people are starting to look at us, Mit. And my family's starting to notice."

"Don't make me choose, Kháll. Don't make me choose sculpting or you. I don't want to have to make that choice."

"There are leaves of absence, aren't there? How long can you take?"

"Probably about two months, but then I wouldn't be

able to get sick for the rest of the year. And it wouldn't look good—"

"Please. Read Tymó's... whatever it is, and then tell me if you think it isn't worth trying to find him. If he was twenty-five years old twenty-one years ago then he's probably still alive."

Mitri released an 'I can't believe I'm considering this' sigh, pulled himself up out of Kháll's grasp and off the cot, then walked to his workbench, where he ignited a lantern to push back the ever-encroaching darkness, and opened the gilded, green box. Kháll got up and stood by his side, reading with him.

Kháll had been on ships before, but only for day trips to and from the Gnoss peninsula. And those had been far more luxurious. He hadn't told anyone he was leaving, and Mitri had only requested of his masters in the Sculptor's Guild an extended leave. Unable to afford the comforts of the commercial vessels that frequented the peninsula, they'd settled for a small room, barely more than a closet, on a cargo trawler, the entire inside of which reeked of olive oil, the primary substance of the vessel's trade.

Despite the smell, their cabin was similar to Mitri's work shed in both size and amenities. The similarity was deceptively appealing. They tried to engage in their usual sexual hijinks the first night, only to discover the utter necessity of being near the stream back at home.

217

Kháll went above deck to clean himself and managed to avoid the rest of the crew, but Mitri returned to their cabin red-faced and panting, telling a tale of being spotted by a crew member who'd come up to take a leak while Mitri was washing himself.

After that, there were both much more careful about the kind of fun they engaged in.

The glares from the crew also grew more hostile with every passing day, until they reached the point where each of them was so frightened that merely sat in their room taking turns sleeping.

The thoroughly uncomfortable voyage ended on the morning of it sixth day, and both Kháll and Mitri were glad to leave the vessel.

The port of Meigá was a recognizable kind of place. The dock workers wore similar clothes as the port workers in Sóf, and the buildings were all of similar shapes and sizes. Kháll and Mitri had their papers signed and exited into the streets. Beyond the port, Meigá was a completely different world from Sóf.

The first things Kháll noticed was the streets. Litter and refuse studded ever curb. He watched a man spit onto the pavement. And whenever a sea breeze passed by, which was frequently, the smell of urine seemed to waft into his nostrils from one direction or another.

Sitting at the corners were hooded figures wearing not robes, the clothing of the middle and noble classes in all of Palípoli, but tattered rags. Sóf indeed had some such individuals, but in Meigá, there were as many impoverished sitting near the entrance to the port as Sóf probably had in their entire city.

Khállí and Mitri both watched wide-eyed as a chariot passed, hauled by dirt-strewn individuals who'd been harnessed in to pull it. The man operating the chariot held a whip, and a few of the individuals bore red lacerations.

Khállí gulped. "Let's find the Theater Guild."

Mitri nodded wordlessly, his face oddly blank. Khállí guessed that internally, Mitri was anything but lacking emotion.

The two of them experienced significant trouble getting anyone to stop and give them directions. Most passersby ignored them completely. They ended up wandering into the merchant's district, where vendors refused to engage with them without a purchase. Finally, Khállí gave in and spent a small fortune on a meal of much poorer quality than he could buy for the same price at home, and the cafeteria owner acquiesced to giving him directions to the Theater Guild, and of course, it was on the other side of town completely.

They reached the theater district with only a couple of hours of sunlight left in the day. While all of Sóf's guilds had a kind of splendor to them, some kind of significant architectural flare decided upon by how the city's founding architects had decided to best represent the glory of the gods on Earth, the Theater Guild of Sóf was nothing more than a wooden box without windows.

They stepped inside a dingy foyer to discover a young man their own age reading a scroll. He didn't look up, even after Kháll cleared his throat.

"Excuse me," Kháll said.

The young man finally turned up from his scroll. "Hey."

"Hi." Kháll did his best to keep is voice level. "We'd like to consult the guild's archive."

The young man lifted an eyebrow. "Archive?"

Kháll and Mitri shared a glance.

"You do keep records of who your members are over time, or your interactions with the council and other guilds, right?"

"Oh," the young man said. "Those are all in the cellar. They don't have a master."

Kháll blinked. "All your records… are just sitting in the cellar, unattended?"

"Uh, yeah…" The young man turned back to his scroll.

"Have you ever heard of Synai Tymó?" Kháll asked.

The young man's chest slumped and he expelled an exasperated sigh. "No—" His tone began with exasperation and then morphed to curiosity. "That name sure does sound familiar though."

"He'd be in his mid-forties now," Mitri added. "We think he came to Meigá twenty years ago."

The young man grinned and nodded. "Tell me,

what's your relationship to him?"

Kháll looked to Mitri, who he considered to be much better at handling these kinds of questions.

"We're just interested in finding out what happened to him after he left Sóf," Mitri said.

The young man grinned and nodded. He reached under his desk and retrieve two green coins, not the usual ruddy brown copper color of regular currency. He reached out and placed one in each of their hands.

"These will get you into the tonight's play. But don't let the gatemaster take them. After the show, hand them over the guys guarding the stage, and they'll take you in back. Ask for Enkei." The young man's grin grew wide. "He'll be able to tell you all about Synai."

The guild attendant's green coins worked like a charm. The gatekeeper did indeed try to take them, but when Kháll and Mitri insisted on keeping them, the gatekeeper relented and ushered them inside the theater.

Unlike the Theater Guild, the theater itself was an orate and heavily embellished building, but, Kháll remarked to himself, not the same kind of style and attention to detail such a building would receive in Sóf. There was something overdone and impractical about the design stylings of this building, the arches within and arches and the geometric figured carved into stone. It was as though the architect had sensed that the building *should have* style, but had lacked any sense of what *con-*

stituted good or bad style.

They found seats quickly enough, and only minutes later, the play began.

At first, the actors were all young people, their age, and they worried that this Enkei fellow would not actually appear in the play, but in the middle of the second act, a tall, older gentleman with a gray beard trotted onto the stage in robes of a style from three generations prior. He affected a booming, grandiose demeanor for the sake of his character, and Kháll knew at once that he was watching Enkei.

After the performance, they waited for the auditorium to empty, and when enough room down the aisles opened up, they hurried toward the door at the side of the stage. They held up their green coins to the guard, and he nodded. Kháll and Mitri pulled open the door, and shuffled inside.

Behind the stage, all of the veneer of the third wall fell away. Actors walked about, talking as themselves rather than their characters, and in only fragments of their costumes. Theater assistants who were not actors affected changes to the placement of props on the stage. Other attendants blew out the candles suspended above, and the stage lay half shrouded in darkness.

"Can I help you?" A booming voice said beside them, and both Kháll and Mitri started. They turned to see the tall, older man standing beside them.

Kháll gulped. "Are you Enkei?"

"Yes," he said, furrowing his brow in mild concern. "And you are?"

"I'm Khâll."

"And I'm Mitri. We're from Sóf."

Enkei raised his eyebrows at the news of their origin. "How can I help you?"

"We heard," Mitri said, "that you can give us some information we're looking for. We're trying to discover the whereabouts of a man named Synai Tymó."

Enkei's face twisted up in the most gruesome expression, as though he'd just been forced to swallow sour milk.

"We're sorry," Khâll tried. "We didn't mean to upset you. We're just trying to find him. We just want to talk to him."

Enkei released a sigh. "He relocated to Kholumv."

Khâll's heart fell. He looked to Mitri, who pursed his lips and swallowed.

"When was this?" Khâll asked.

"Twelve years ago."

"Did he get a position within their Theater Guild?"

Enkei chortled. "Kholumv doesn't have a Theater Guild."

"Then what profession did he take up?" Mitri asked. "He wasn't taken into slavery, was he?"

"Gods," Enkei laughed. "I wish. I don't know what profession he took up. I don't know what he did for work after twelve years ago. He burned every bridge he had in this guild, though. I doubt anyone here would vouch for him. He was a lousy playwright and a terrible actor. About all he was good at was telling other people what he thought their failings were."

Khǎll and Mitri shared another glance. "We were told you would be able to tell us about him. If everyone in the guild hated him and no one respected him, then what's you're connection—"

"He married my ex-wife," Enkei hissed with unrestrained vitriol. "She was originally from Kholumv. After they married, they both moved there. I don't know what happened to either of them after that." The pain in his voice was evident alongside the anger.

"Thank you," Mitri said.

Khǎll nodded. "This was really helpful. Sorry to dredge up your past."

Enkei nodded curtly and walked off.

Khǎll and Mitri both exited the theater as quickly as their feet could take them.

Khǎll and Mitri left the theater and walked toward the business district in silence.

Khǎll had not expected this. He'd prepared himself to find out that Synai was dead, or that he had achieve an echelon of power that had rendered him unreachable. Whatever outcome he had imagined, Meigǎ had been the terminus of his adventure, not a way station.

Yet another move? Mitri was already uncomfortable.

Their situation degraded as the evening wore on. Hotel after hotel after youth hostel after rundown bungalow refused to sell them a room, and not for lack of money, but because two men their age sharing a room could only mean one thing, and the proprietors of Meigá didn't want that kind of association anywhere near their establishments, even the ones that quietly accommodated prostitution.

Kháll and Mitri, in the wee hours of the morning, eventually gave up and walked to the dock, passing hordes of shackled slaves, some attached to chariots, others not, but all certainly off to some grueling task or another.

At the dock, they booked cheap passage on a cargo ship to Kholumv leaving at dawn, then asked where they might wait for the departure. The dock attendant showed them to a small room at the edge of the dock, a foyer to a supply room that contained a small bench.

Kháll slumped against the wall, and Mitri slumped against him. Mitri offered to keep the first watch, but Kháll said he would be the one to stay awake.

"Wake me up in two hours," Mitri suggested.

The two hours came and went, but Kháll let him sleep. He sat, watching the sun come up, just at the edge of the horizon he could see from his perch on the Meigá dock bench, and he thought about Perip and his taming of the great sea beasts of the northeastern seas.

A barge drifted into the dock, and it was only when

the dock workers started unloading it that Kháll started from his reverie and woke Mitri. They pulled themselves up off the bench, grabbed up their things, and the two of them shuffled toward the cargo ship that would take them to Kholumv.

It was a bit bigger than the ship that had brought them to Meigá, but their quarters were a near identical match for their first. No sooner had the captain shown them in and closed the door, than they both fell onto the dingy cot which smelled of soot and grime, and they were asleep once more.

In the days that followed, Kháll and Mitri hardly talked, and they didn't engage in any sexual activities at all. In fact, they barely touched one another at all, which Kháll found disconcerting and uncomfortable after spending so much time growing close. He wanted to either verbally or physically reach out, but he didn't do either. He remained physically chaste because he worried about instigating violence from the crew of the ship, as had nearly happened on the first voyage. Who knew what had been seen or overheard and become common gossip amongst that crew?

As for why they no longer talked, he couldn't tell. They had always had sculpture or poetry to talk about before, but there was nothing to sculpt at sea, nor any paper on which to write—only the scrolls which held Synai Tymó's story. The journey had taken away all their common referents, all the things that brought them close lay thousands of mettrs distant.

Kháll himself was growing weary of sailing, as well. It upset his digestion, and left him in a foul mood for most of the days and nights.

After nine days of fitful sleep and awkward silence, the crew announced that the ship was docking in Kholumv port. The only bit of joy at this for Kháll was the hope that he could meet finally meet Synai, close this chapter of his life, and get on with poetry. The more distant his humiliation before the reading auditions grew, the more it tugged at his heart and soul not to be writing.

Kháll and Mitri sloughed through the port and got their papers signed, the whole time Kháll wondering why it was that ports should look the same all across Palípoli. As they exited into the streets of Kholumv, they found themselves with yet another perspective on city design. Unlike Sóf and Meigá, the primary component of architecture was sandstone, and their terrain, in stark contrast to the rolling hills of their home city, was completely flat. The road stretched out straight before them, and as far as they could see left and right. The streets seemed to form a perfect grid.

And as for the citizens, they noticed a lot fewer robes than they were used to. Groups of soldiers marched passed, as numerous or perhaps more numerous than the robed builders, crafters, and politicians. There were clearly two castes: one went about bare-chested, wearing only shorts and with sheathed swords strapped to their backs, and the other wore heavy metal armor and carried long, forked pikes. Kháll wondered how they could possibly be comfortable under all that armor in the hot summer sun, which seemed even warmer here than in either Sóf or Meigá.

At least it was much easier to get directions than in Meigá. The soldiers were eminently helpful, seeming to view polite direction-giving as a part of their public service. Although some of them eyed Kháll and Mitri in a way that made Kháll uncomfortable.

They found their way to the city council hall, the grandest sandstone building Kháll had ever seen. It had huge stairs leading up to a central meeting area surrounded by columns. The bureaucrats here were also eminently helpful, and it was not long before they found themselves underground in a cavern lined with lanterns.

They passed through a gate, and an elderly man sat at a desk in front of many rows of shelves lined with wooden crates.

"Hello," Kháll said. "We'd like to know where we can find Mr. and Mrs. Synai Tymó."

The old man briefly licked his lips and looked inquisitively over their shoulder momentarily. "Sounds familiar."

He turned and walked back into his shelves. Kháll and Mitri hesitantly followed him, and then strode more confidently after him when it became clear that he wouldn't send them away.

"Tymó…" the man said as his finger scanned the labels of the boxes. "Tymó… Tymó… Aha!"

He pulled at a box with more strength than Kháll would expect from a man of his age and pulled out parcels of bound papers from it.

"Got it. Synai Tymó. Moved here twelve years ago, it looks like. Sold his home and left the island four years ago."

Kháll's heart dropped. He looked at Mitri, but his face was unreadable, a complete blank slate. Whatever Mitri was feeling, he was hiding it, but Kháll didn't need to read his face. He knew his friend well enough. Mitri would not follow him to Synai's next home.

"Where can we find Mrs. Synai Tymó?" Mitri asked, to Kháll's surprise.

"The former," the old man said. "I remember him now. There was a big uproar around his designs for the new stadium five years ago. It went on for months in the council. After dragging it out for over a year, as I recall, he told off the city council and left the island, abandoning his wife, who he'd fallen out with."

"Do you know where to?" Kháll asked.

The man nodded. "They say he boarded a ship for Khatap. The story is that a particular council member hated him so much, he sabotaged the ship so it would sink. But another council member found out and warned the captain in time. To my knowledge, that ship made it to Khatap safe and sound, unless something else happened later in its voyage."

Kháll felt woozy. A trip from Kholumv to Khatap would take ten to eleven days, and all the rest of his money.

He thanked the old man for his time, and he and Mitri walked silently back toward the port. Halfway there, they spotted a public garden, and Kháll suggested they take a break. They walked amongst the grass and trees until they found a bench. Mitri sat without any prompting, and Kháll sat beside him.

Birds sang in the trees behind them. They both seemed to want some silence before the conversation they knew they were about to have.

"You're going to Khatap, aren't you." Mitri broke the silence first, his question sounding like a statement, without any intonation whatsoever.

"Yeah."

"You realize you won't have enough money after that to get back to Sóf."

"There'll be some ship eventually that I can row on. I'm strong enough to row."

Mitri looked at him with fearful eyes. He didn't have to say it. Both of them knew that there was a chance, and not a small one, that if the captain of such a ship was of a mind to, he could end up selling Kháll into slavery and making sure his owner got told never to take him anywhere near Sóf.

"This means *that* much to you?"

"Yeah."

Mitri blinked at him, disbelievingly. "Khâll, I'm beginning to believe that the guy we've be tracking across the archipelago didn't actually write those scrolls." He held out his hand, ticking off items on his fingers. "One, he got himself banned from our Poets' Guild. Two, he pisses off everyone in the Meigá Theater Guild and steals a guy's wife. Three, he pisses off the city council of Kholumv badly enough that someone tried to murder a boatful of innocent people just to get revenge on him. Is this really a person that you're willing to risk—" he dropped his volume. "—*slavery* for? What the hell would your parents say? I'd probably agree with them on this one!"

Khâll pulled out the green box, and carefully pried open the lid. He looked at the old, worn, browned paper of the scrolls, each with their little red ribbons. Care, craftsmanship, and love had gone into making them. It was so terribly apparent. Mitri was right. Some kind of disconnect did clearly exist.

"You could be right," Khâll said. "But there's another possibility."

"Oh?"

"Something might have happened to him on Sôf, after he wrote these scrolls but before all the nastiness that proceeded in his life, something that changed him, ruined him." Khâll held out the box before him. "This is who I want to become. The person who can create *this*."

Kháll clasped the green box harder. "Not exactly this, but stuff like it. If pursuing this turns you into the man whose life we've been following…" Kháll shook his head. "I have to keep going. To the end. Even knowing the risks."

Mitri bit his lip. "You know I have to go back to Sóf."

"Yeah."

"I thought so."

"Mitri?"

A long moment of silence passed, with just the sound of the wind and the birds chirping in the trees. Kháll glanced about them, seeing if other people were anywhere near. He saw no one.

He turned to Mitri, looked in his eyes, and silently mouthed the words, *I love you*.

Mitri gulped and water appeared at the brims of his eyes. Kháll's own eyes were watering, too.

I love you, too. Mitri's lips also moved without sound.

Kháll and Mitri bought separate tickets but walked together the waiting area of the dock.

They did not speak.

Mitri's vessel back to Sóf arrived first, as was announced by the dock attendant for the Kholumv port waiting room. They seemed better staffed for visitors than Meigá, probably because of the yearly inter-city games.

Mitri stood, walked to the door, looked back at

Kháll, and smiled weakly. Kháll gulped and did his best to smile. And then, seemingly all at once, Mitri was out the door and gone.

Kháll fell into a fugue state. He moved from the waiting room to his vessel to his cramped quarters to the deck of the cargo ship without gaining an awareness of how each of the moments was connected to any of the others. He only sensed deeply that some anchor, some integral part of his life was now torn away from him, and he'd become unhinged. His captain surely knew their ship's course and speed, but Kháll himself was adrift.

He spent his days aboard the ship either reading *Peripesus*, or rubbing his purse and its four meager coins between its fingers. He would arrive safely at Khatap, but what then? He knew only a little of the island. It was supposedly the most backwater of all the major Palípolian powers. Thet were primarily a farming community. They exported wool and textiles. They imported dyes from Fid.

That was it.

He could not imagine choosing to stay there after all the effort he expended to find Synai Tymó. He expected the conclusion would be that Tymó was dead, or that he had moved yet again, or that he had sailed off toward the horizon and was never heard from again.

On the sixth day of the voyage, he found himself reading *Peripesus* and wondering just what it was that had excited him so much on his first reading. It fascinated him how, upon the second and third readings, the work taught him something new each time. But now, as he was on his sixth, seventh, or eighth (he had lost count), he was growing rather sick of it. He wished for something else. Hell, he would even read Pragog's fart poem if it were available to him, if only to break the monotony.

It struck him all at once—the same text, no matter how well-crafted, had its limits. This was why they had libraries, and Poets' Guilds, and why they studied poetics broadly. A single text by itself could not sustain an artist, or any sensitive human being. Texts existed together, dancing together on the stage of the world.

Here, at sea, his heart was starving. He'd already torn himself away from the most important person in his life to be out here, and now, he realized, he didn't even have an artistic community to draw on, either. And all because he needed to find Tymó.

The days wore on, and still he read *Peripesus* again and again, mentally noting all the of the observations of the text he would write down later. His analysis had grown quite complex. Were he admitted to the Sófan Poets' Guild at this moment, he'd be able to draft his analytical thesis within days, an effort that took most initiates the better part of a year. Not that any Poets' Guild masters would probably accept Tymó's work as legitimate.

Just after noon on the eleventh day of the voyage, a knock sounded on the door to Kháll's cabin.

"Yes?" he called.

The captain opened the door and peered inside. "We've docked at Khatap port. Get your things."

He closed the cabin door without waiting for Kháll to reply.

Kháll carefully repackaged the scrolls in their green box, took it and his pack, and left the ship.

Khatap's port was just like all the others. He walked amongst the crates and carts and sweaty dock workers toward the exit. He had his papers signed and walked out into the plaza beyond the gates.

He gathered enough about his environs to note a provincial quality to the architecture and streets, but he found himself uninterested in their details. He turned his attention to the people. People hurried by, all of them wearing robes of one color or another. They all looked rather busy.

At last he spotted a group of people standing in the center of the plaza with starry, faraway looks in their eyes. One was an older man, another one about Kháll's own age, and then there was a middle-aged couple, the husband wearing robes adorned with silver stitching. Kháll wondered what his position in the city council was.

None of them looked to be hurrying anywhere.

"Excuse me," Kháll called as he approached them, "Could you possibly help me? I'm a visitor from Sóf, and I've come in search of someone."

The group turned to him, and their starry, faraway look faded, replaced with surprise. Kháll at first wondered if he'd interrupted a group in mourning of some kind, but then the oldest man spoke. "We don't get a lot of visitors from Sóf. My name's Anatix. And you are?"

"My name's Kháll."

"Hi, Kháll," the young man said.

The older man smiled. "Welcome to Khatap. Who can we help you find?"

"His name is Synai Tymó."

The well-dressed man let out a derisive laugh.

"He's dead, isn't he?" Kháll said.

"No," the well-dressed man replied. "Though I know a lot of people on the council who wish he was."

"He's... here?" Kháll's eyes widened.

Anatix nodded, and raised an eyebrow. "Why are you looking for him?"

"I just need to talk to him," Kháll said, more sheepishly than he'd intended.

"Fíl..." Anatix cast his solemn gaze at the young man.

The young man, suddenly animated, nodded back.

"I can find the way myself," Kháll said. "I don't want to be a bother."

"It's no problem," Fíl and the well-dressed man said at the same time.

The well-dressed man nodded to Fíl.

"Come on," Fíl said, and he started across the plaza.

"Stop by later, Fíl," the woman called to him.

"Will do, Mrs. Makhaino," Fíl called back.

Kháll followed him down the streets. He looked like a pretty fit guy, kind of skinny, probably a runner. Cute face, though. Fond memories of Mitri flowed back to him.

"What brings you all the way from Sóf?" Fíl asked.

He briefly entertained the notion of continuing the secret of Tymó's writings, but decided that this was the moment for admission. He could not let himself get this close only to have the offer of help retracted. "Some... writings."

"Writings? What, stuff you wrote? Or stuff Tymó wrote?"

"Tymó's writings."

They passed under a large stone archway. The city streets changed to a dirt roads, and clusters of homes and shops became demarcated blocks of farmland. Onward they strode.

"You liked it?"

"Yeah."

"Have you ever met him?"

"Nope."

"You must have really liked his writing, if you came all this way."

Kháll nodded. He felt the admission of his letting go of Mitri struggling to burst forth, but he held it back. He just didn't know Fíl well enough.

"I gave up a lot to come out here to find him. And I heard about Tymó's life along the way... Well, I hope I at least get the answers I'm looking for."

A long silence passed between them. All around them, in the fields beyond the road, the sound of scythes hacking away at wheat and barley, the subtle thrashing noise of hewn plant matter erupting all around them at uneven intervals.

"My best friend got on a ship and left the island today," Fíl said.

Kháll momentarily didn't know how to respond. "That must have been really rough."

"I mean, it's not like he'll never come back. It just... it sucks, is all."

"Where'd he go?"

"Épanngel. Got a job there."

"Ah. You could get a job there too, probably."

Fíl shook his head in a way that suggested to Kháll he should not pursue that line of questioning.

Soon the farmland dissipated, replaced by empty grasslands dotted with hills which grew into rocky mountains in the distance.

"How far out does Tymó live?"

"Past Anatix's place."

"And where's that?"

Patches of grass and sand appeared in the dirt path.

"Just a little further this way."

They rounded a bend and passed a small cabin built just past the spot where the sandy beach turned to dirt. A circle of charred firewood sat in the middle of the sand.

"Does Tymó get along with anyone on Khatap?"

Kháll asked.

Fíl shook his head.

"Does he still write?"

Fíl shrugged.

It made sense. If no one liked him, who would want to read any of his writing?

They rounded another bend, and another hut came into view, this one not as well maintained as the one belonging to Anatix. Parts of the roof were moldy and caving in, and the grasses near the hut hadn't been cut back.

Fíl and Kháll approached the door. Fíl cast a questioning glance at Kháll, who nodded his approval.

Fíl knocked.

"Who is it?" a deep, crackly baritone voice called from inside.

"Fíl."

"What do you want?"

Fíl rolled his eyes. "You have a visitor from Sóf."

A moment's silence. Then the sound of footsteps. The door opened.

A man stood before them, a bit shorter than Kháll. He had wide shoulders, long black hair and thick curly beard that was rather unkempt. His robes were clean enough for someone who lived alone, Kháll supposed, but then there were his eyes. Kháll very much disliked the feeling he got from looking into Synai's eyes.

Synai Tymó looked Kháll up and down. "Do I know you?"

Kháll swallowed his fear. "My parents bought my house from your parents sixteen years ago."

Synai blinked, and his eyes locked onto the green box Kháll held in his hands.

Kháll took a deep breath. "I found *Peripesus*, and I read it. About two dozen times. I want to know what you call this kind of writing, and what inspired it."

Tymó's eyes moved between the box and Kháll's eyes. Again and again, his eyes darted, until they landed at last on Kháll's face and stayed their. "You're serious?"

"Yes."

"You crossed a hundred thousand mettrs of sea to find me so you could ask me about a mangled corpse of sloppy writing I produced in my twenties?"

Kháll pursed his lips. Fíl sighed and leaned into the door frame.

"Do you know what the Poets' Guild did when I read the first scroll of *Peripesus* at an audition?"

Kháll returned Tymó's gaze blankly and silently.

"They laughed me off the stage. They laughed *me* off the stage. Do you have any idea what that feels like?"

Kháll didn't dare respond in the affirmative, despite wanting to.

"And here you are, twenty years later, some punk who thinks he's found something special. Here are the only things you need to know about *Peripesus*. First, and most importantly, it's garbage. The reason that I stuffed it under my floorboards was not because I wanted it to be discovered. It is not buried treasure, or anything even remotely romantic. I buried it because because it was dead, a corpse. It was dead to me then, and it's dead to me now. My only mistake was not burning it, which in hindsight would have been a more fitting end, and would have prevented this awful moment, the present awkward idiocy which you have thrust upon us both."

Fíl crossed his arms. "Why didn't you burn it then?"

Tymó scoffed. "My idiot brother. Something about it being unholy to burn writing of any kind. He's a priest, so go figure."

Kháll felt emotionally gutted, abused on the deepest level. He realized he was looking at the ground, so instead he looked up into Synai Tymó's eyes once more. "Is there any part of you that still thinks *Peripesus* has value?"

"No," Tymó said. "If the master or journeymen of the Sóf Poets' Guild had had the foresight and recognition and see what it was in its time, then it would have had value, but the true proof of its worthlessness is that the only person to find any meaning in it is an unapprenticed, unskilled, idiot kid who was stupid enough to waste months of his life crossing tracts of sea to find its writer. You are the only person in existence who thinks this has value. And that is proof of the fact that it has none."

Kháll found his emotions swirling. Just weeks ago, he would have lashed out and replied with vitriolic rage.

He would have been sure he was right. He found he wasn't sure of much of anything anymore.

Well, he realized, perhaps one thing.

He leaned over and set the green box down at Tymó's feet.

"Thank you," Khǎll said.

Tymó frowned, turned, and slammed the door to his hut in Khǎll and Fíl's faces, which in turn tipped over the box and caused the scrolls to spill out onto the dirt.

"Let's go," Khǎll said.

"That's it?" Fíl asked as they began away.

"That's it."

"What about the poem?"

Khǎll licked his lips and pondered the decision, just to be certain. Yes. He was certain, at least about this. "I learned what I needed from it. I don't need it anymore."

Khǎll shambled forward in a bleary, uncertain daze, only vaguely aware of Fíl's presence at his side.

All at once, Khǎll noticed Fíl burst into a sprint, and away. "Hey, Khǎll!" Fíl called out. "Over here!"

Khǎll glanced about his surroundings and realized that they'd returned to the house of the man called Anatix. With a deep sigh, a great expelling of negative energy, he walked to where Fíl stood beside Anatix's hut. Fíl opened up an enormous crate and was pulling out foodstuffs—bread and some cheese.

"Isn't this Anatix's hut?"

Fíl grinned. "He won't mind. I promise it isn't stealing."

"I appreciate what you're trying to do, but really—"

"Follow me," Fíl said.

Realizing he had no other viable options, Kháll followed Fíl and his armful of bread and cheese to a path in
the back of Anatix's hut. It led into the rocky hills, and
rose sharply upward for many hundred mettrs, until finally flattening out into a small mountain peak. They
came to a stop at the edge of a shear cliff, where Fíl sat,
letting his legs hang off the edge. He set the food down
beside him.

"You hungry?" Fíl tore into the bread and handed
over half of a loaf.

Kháll felt weary all over, both physically tired and
emotionally spent. Part of him wanted to say that he
wasn't, be he realized that would be both rude and a lie.
He took the bread. "Thanks."

Kháll sat down and looked out over Khatap. It looked
even smaller from above. But he had to admit, it was a
beautiful city. If it weren't for his family back at home, he
might not actually mind being stuck here. He'd try to get
back, for them. But perhaps he'd let himself enjoy this,
for just a little while anyway.

"I'll bet you're sorry you came all this way to meet
Tymó," Fíl said.

Kháll shook his head.

"Really?"

"Yeah. He taught me something important."

"What's that?"

"The writer's attitude is as important as the writing. The writing won't mean anything if the writer is a terrible human being."

"Did you really think his poems were that good?"

Khráll nodded. "He had a lot of potential. But he threw it away because he wanted attention and praise more than he wanted to create something beautiful."

"I think I heard one of the weavers say something like that once."

Khráll smiled. "My sisters love Khatap quilts. Aega has one for every season."

"Man, just think about that." Fíl looked out at Khatap. "Thousands of mettrs away there are people who have stuff that came from people born and raised on Khatap. I'll bet all the cities have some connection like this."

A long silence passed.

"I lost my best friend recently, too." The suddenness of Khráll's words surprised even him. He grabbed up some bread and cheese and stuffed them in his mouth, mostly to prevent himself from saying something else stupid.

"What happened?" Fíl asked.

Khráll swallowed. "He ran out of money and decided to go back to Sóf without me."

"So, he'll be there when you get back, right?"

Khráll didn't respond.

"You're going back, right?"

"Yeah."

"Arkh went to Épanngel and I don't know if he's ever coming back or not. I mean, he probably will, to see his parents, but who knows how often he'll get to do that. What's your friend's name?"

"Mitri."

"The next time Arkh's at home, you two should come here, and we could all hang out. That would be fun."

Kháll smiled at that. "It would. We should try to figure out how to do that."

This is how you try to conceal loneliness, Kháll thought, and realized it was something they were both doing. He wondered if Fíl noticed.

They sat on the mountain some time longer, sharing stories of Khatap, Sóf, Meigá, and Kholumv.

Fíl and his mother had already planned to have dinner with Arkh's parents, and of course, they invited Kháll. He got to tell the whole story of finding Tymó's poem and his subsequent journey across Palípoli all over again. The Makhainos bristled at the description of Tymó's behavior earlier that day, and were aghast that a visitor to their island had been poorly treated.

"Tymó's not welcome in the city," Arkh's father kept saying.

When they finally broached the subject of Kháll's return trip, he found the questioning prevented him from avoiding the topic he wished to conceal—his financial status.

Mr. Makhaino insisted on paying Kháll's way.

"Mr. Makhaino, I really couldn't—"

"I have terms of payment." He folded his hands. "One poem, composed specifically for my family, to be mailed directly to me within a month of your return. And, I wish for you to give us a tour of Sóf the next time we visit your city."

It took Kháll many moments to realize his mouth was hanging open. He was glad he hadn't had food in it. Eventually, he regained his composure, and after much befuddled rambling, managed to agree to Mr. Makhaino's terms.

He slept in the room Arkh had vacated just the night prior, and Kháll found himself, just before lying down, looking over all the things Arkh had owned in his previous life—a lot of pencils, diagraming equipment, story scrolls, some clothes (probably the ones that didn't fit him anymore), even a couple of books, which must have been on loan from the city hall (probably the result of Mr. Makhaino's connections).

Kháll fell asleep wondering what it was like to be an engineer instead of an artist. Could someone be both? That would be an interesting character for a narrative of the kind Tymó had invented.

The next day, Arkh's family took him to the dock

and bought him passage to Sóf on a rather expensive commercial vessel that would stop at Fid on its way. Worried that he would stand out like a sore thumb amidst dignitaries and councilmen, he tried to talk Mr. Makhaino into a cargo vessel, but Arkh's father would have it no other way. Luxury boat it was.

He said goodbye, promised he would write, and settled in for a very leisurely cruise home. When he got to his room and opened up his pack upon his very soft-looking bed draped with fancy covers and lined with cushions, he discovered a package he didn't recognize. A note was taped to it: "So you can get a head start on your payback. - Fíl"

Within the package was a stack of paper, an inkwell, and a quill.

Kháll spent every day of the voyage writing, and made a point of sitting on the deck to do so whenever it wasn't too windy.

By the time his ship docked at Sóf, he had written fourteen poems, five of which he immediately copied and mailed to the Makhainos, and four of which were narratives in the style Tymó had invented. Kháll's protagonist, instead of the adventuring, beast-slaughtering captain, was an engineer and artist, struggling to find his way in a world that insisted he choose one guild or the other.

Stepping off the ship into Sóf port was one of the most surreal experiences of his life. Meigá, Kholumv and Khatap had all seemed strange, but that strangeness could not compare to the oddity of seeing his home city, the place he had known all his life, in a completely different way. The streets and buildings were the same, but also somehow new.

As he drew closer to his home, his attention turned to the upcoming discussion with his parents. He found himself oddly prepared for it, however, and it turned out to be in fact quite easy, but as that conversation came to its close, the thought of finding Mitri overshadowed everything else.

Best to find out where they stood and get it over with, he decided. He walked resolutely through the city, beyond the gates, and away, all the time marveling at the novel-sameness of everything around him.

Kháll found Mitri working at a stone carving in the front yard of his house. Mitri smiled, and the two of them hugged, then shared stories of their time apart. Kháll decided to save talk of their relationship, whatever it was, for later. Perhaps they would have to get married. Perhaps not. He still loved Mitri, and that would never change. At last, he invited Mitri to see him audition at the Poets' Guild that night.

"Really?" Mitri asked incredulously. "After everything Tymó said?"

"Especially after everything Tymó said," Kháll responded calmly.

Mitri gave an impressed and very cute smirk, then sent Kháll on his way.

Kháll went home and spent the rest of the day going over and over the narratives he'd created. He eventually chose one story, and one poem, which he decided would be a backup in case he lost his nerve, but he would try his best not to.

After the sun set, he found himself all nerves. He walked down the streets gripping his papers tightly. He thought about having to go back to the press and beg for his job back. He thought about being asked to step down from the podium again—and realized he didn't care. His writing was valuable to him, and it always would be. He could explain its worth to anyone who asked, and he would tell anyone who showed interest in it how proud he was of it. He would try to learn what it was they had gleaned from it. Even if what they gleaned was negative. Those were joyous moments to be treasured, not reviled or disparaged.

He walked into the auditorium of the Poets' Guild and found Mitri, already sitting in the fourth row from the front, the same place they had been so many weeks ago.

Kháll lost himself to the poems of others, turning them all over in his mind. What did they mean to him? What were the authors here trying to express? Some of them weren't trying to express anything, but that was fine. Enough of them were.

"Next on the list," the journeyman proctor said, "is Kháll Anaklypsi."

249

Kháll stood, and walked to the podium. "Good evening," he said, in his loudest, most confident voice. "I recently came back from a long trip, to Meigá, Kholumv, and finally Khatap. I took this trip so that I could learn more about a new art form I discovered. It's something quite novel. If you'll indulge me, I'd like to share a short piece I've written in that style. And if it resonates with you, I hope you'll tell me how and why."

NOTES

One day at writing group, I found myself sketching out an archipelago instead of writing. That map would eventually become the world of Palípoli, an iron-age civilization similar to fifth century Greece.

With *Schrödinger's City*, I realized that I'd been unconsciously populating my fictional worlds with fewer and fewer fantastic elements, all while attempting to maximize the effectiveness of those elements.

When I started thinking about what I wanted the world of Palípoli to be like, I was fully aware of this tendency, and I decided I wanted to push that boundary as far as I could. The result was that the world of Palípoli differs from ours in that it has three moons rather than one. Palípoli has no system of magic, there are no fantastic creatures, and while the characters may believe in the intervention of various deities in their world, the happenings described in the stories (to the extent that their narrators can be trusted) are explicable with our own contemporary systems of science and rational logic.

However, the fictional potential of this seemingly tiny change of three moons was enormous. From it, I was able to extrapolate and play with systems of religion, ethics, and culture that would not have been possible otherwise. "The Measure" is the best example of this principle driving a crucial element of the story.

In other cases, such as "Simple Reason" and "Rite of Courage," I drew on my knowledge of the Classical Greek world as a source for Palípoli. In the case of "Simple Reason," it was the Bronze Age Collapse, the environmental impact of deforestation, and ancient irrigation practices. In the case of "Rite of Courage," it was Aeschylus's *Oresteia*.

I wrote "Something Novel" after a particularly irksome reading event, in which I was asked offstage in the middle of my story so that there would be time for the primary reader, whose story, it turned out, was about the vomiting of a cake. "Something Novel" is a reaffirmation of why I write, who I am writing for, and what kind of writer I strive to be. I wanted to show myself the danger of living with the kind of emotional outlook that Khǎll embodies at the beginning of the story, and which Tymó maintains to his end.

And that leaves "The Shipwright."

When I began "The Shipwright," I imagined it as a sprawling novel, in which my journey through professional software engineering would be overlaid onto the context of ancient ship engineering. Arkh was to go to Épanngel and become ensnared in guild politics roughly analogous to my early experiences with large corporations.

However, when Arkh left Khatap, I found the story felt surprisingly complete. I had made the imminence of his departure so fraught that the resolution seemed enough for one story. And I had established the workings of an interesting new world as well.

I am looking forward to many more short stories, novellas, and also novels set in Palípoli.

As it happens, I have been reading recently on the history of science fiction and fantasy. Some scholars want to put the beginning of both genres in the nineteenth century, while others argue for a much longer tradition, stretching back to the Classical world.

I would argue that, if science fiction and fantasy are truly going to be about something, they must reject the isolationist notion that they are something "special," sitting apart from literature and history, a culture of their own. Science fiction and fantasy bring so much literary potential to literature, and in order to realize that potential, science fiction and fantasy writers and readers must be cognizant of our sprawling cultural heritage. We must cognize ourselves as contributors to the literary, rather than pushing back on institutions or individuals who say ignorant things about genres of the fantastic.

I hope that "The Shipwright" and all my other Palípoli stories, in this collection and yet to come, do something, even something small, to help bind science fiction and fantasy to broader literary contexts.

TIME AND LUNAR CYCLES

DAYS OF THE WEEK

There are six days in a Palípolian week. Those days are Féngday, Dasday, Asterday, Thálday, Chryday, and Amnday. The first Féngday of a month is instead called Khorday. However, these names constitute only one system of naming days. Days can also be referred to in terms of which of the three moons appear in the sky. That category of names is called "moonnames," see below).

MOONS

The three moons are Isórrop, Stathro, and Atax. Isórrop is large and white, Stathro is smaller and blue, Atax is close to Stathro in size, but slightly smaller still, and red.

Months & Seasons

There are sixteen months in a Palípolian year and eight seasons. Because they have multiple moons (multiple nearby gravitational forces), their climate fluctuates more than on real world Earth. The months are:

1. Enad (Late Winter)
2. Duad (Late Winter)
3. Traád (Early Spring)
4. Tesserad (Early Spring; growing season starts)
5. Pettad (Early Summer)
6. Eksad (Early Summer)
7. Eptad (Late Spring)
8. Oktad (Late Spring)
9. Ennad (Late Summer)
10. Dékkad (Late Summer)
11. Entékkad (Early Fall)
12. Dudékkad (Early Fall; harvest)
13. Dékkattriad (Early Winter)
14. Dékkatessad (Early Winter)
15. Dékkapettad (Late Fall)
16. Dékkeksad (Late Fall)

Moonnames

Days can also be referred to in terms of which of the moons appears in the sky. A month on Palípoli consists of the three-week cycle in which all three moons will complete one iteration of their appearance pattern (see the calendar at the end of this section). These names for days are called "moonnames." They are:

Ozor (Isórrop only)
Dassr (Stathro only)
Katkási (Atax only)
Ármon (Isórrop and Stathro)
Dikhon (Isórrop and Atax)
Métav (Stathro and Atax)
Makhí (Isórrop, Stathro, and Atax)
Kens (none)

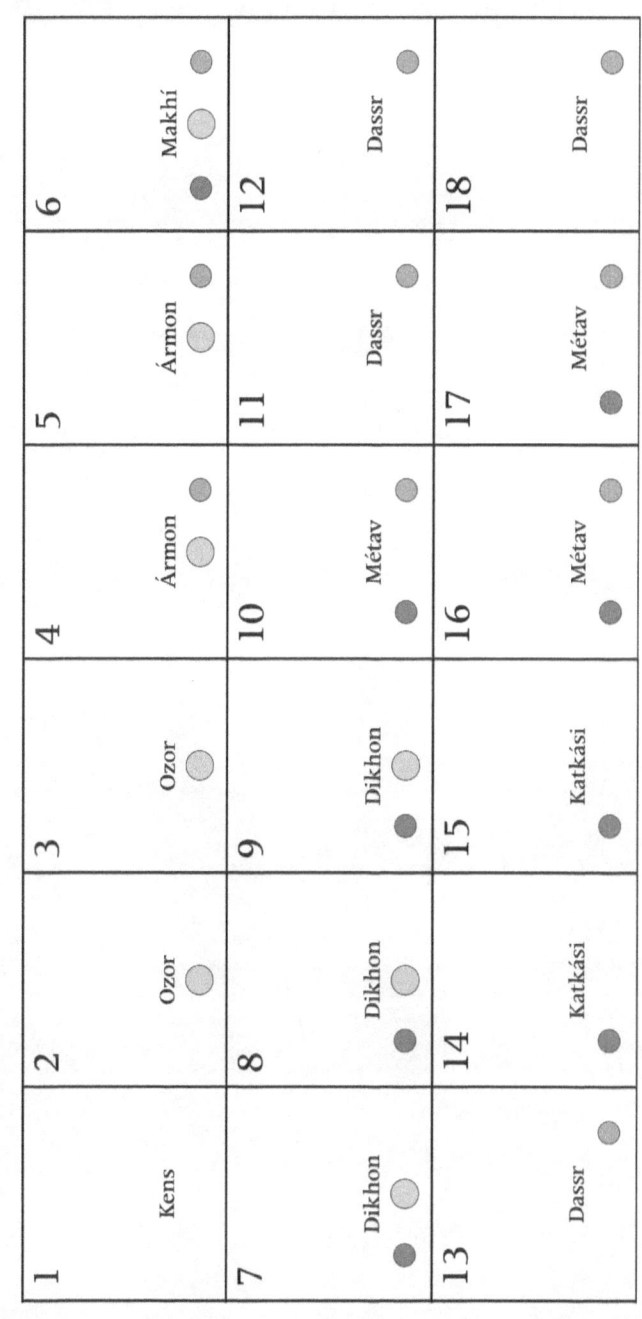

Féngday / Khorday	Dasday	Asterday	Thálday	Chryday	Amnday
1 Kens	2 Ozor	3 Ozor	4 Ármon	5 Ármon	6 Makhí
7 Dikhon	8 Dikhon	9 Dikhon	10 Métav	11 Dassr	12 Dassr
13 Dassr	14 Katkási	15 Katkási	16 Métav	17 Métav	18 Dassr